ALREADY

LOST

(A Laura Frost Suspense Thriller—Book Eight)

BLAKE PIERCE

Blake Pierce

Blake Pierce is the USA Today bestselling author of the RILEY PAGE mystery series, which includes seventeen books. Blake Pierce is also the author of the MACKENZIE WHITE mystery series, comprising fourteen books; of the AVERY BLACK mystery series, comprising six books; of the KERI LOCKE mystery series, comprising five books; of the MAKING OF RILEY PAIGE mystery series, comprising six books; of the KATE WISE mystery series, comprising seven books; of the CHLOE FINE psychological suspense mystery, comprising six books; of the JESSE HUNT psychological suspense thriller series, comprising twenty four books; of the AU PAIR psychological suspense thriller series, comprising three books; of the ZOE PRIME mystery series, comprising six books; of the ADELE SHARP mystery series, comprising sixteen books, of the EUROPEAN VOYAGE cozy mystery series, comprising six books; of the new LAURA FROST FBI suspense thriller, comprising nine books (and counting); of the new ELLA DARK FBI suspense thriller, comprising fourteen books (and counting); of the A YEAR IN EUROPE cozy mystery series, comprising nine books, of the AVA GOLD mystery series, comprising six books (and counting); of the RACHEL GIFT mystery series, comprising eight books (and counting); of the VALERIE LAW mystery series, comprising nine books (and counting); of the PAIGE KING mystery series, comprising six books (and counting); of the MAY MOORE mystery series, comprising nine books (and counting); the CORA SHIELDS mystery series, comprising three books (and counting); and of the NICKY LYONS mystery series, comprising three books (and counting).

An avid reader and lifelong fan of the mystery and thriller genres, Blake loves to hear from you, so please feel free to visit www.blakepierceauthor.com to learn more and stay in touch.

BOOKS BY BLAKE PIERCE

NICKY LYONS MYSTERY SERIES
ALL MINE (Book #1)
ALL HIS (Book #2)
ALL HE SEES (Book #3)

CORA SHIELDS MYSTERY SERIES
UNDONE (Book #1)
UNWANTED (Book #2)
UNHINGED (Book #3)

MAY MOORE SUSPENSE THRILLER
NEVER RUN (Book #1)
NEVER TELL (Book #2)
NEVER LIVE (Book #3)
NEVER HIDE (Book #4)
NEVER FORGIVE (Book #5)
NEVER AGAIN (Book #6)
NEVER LOOK BACK (Book #7)
NEVER FORGET (Book #8)
NEVER LET GO (Book #9)

PAIGE KING MYSTERY SERIES
THE GIRL HE PINED (Book #1)
THE GIRL HE CHOSE (Book #2)
THE GIRL HE TOOK (Book #3)
THE GIRL HE WISHED (Book #4)
THE GIRL HE CROWNED (Book #5)
THE GIRL HE WATCHED (Book #6)

VALERIE LAW MYSTERY SERIES
NO MERCY (Book #1)
NO PITY (Book #2)
NO FEAR (Book #3)
NO SLEEP (Book #4)
NO QUARTER (Book #5)

NO CHANCE (Book #6)
NO REFUGE (Book #7)
NO GRACE (Book #8)
NO ESCAPE (Book #9)

RACHEL GIFT MYSTERY SERIES
HER LAST WISH (Book #1)
HER LAST CHANCE (Book #2)
HER LAST HOPE (Book #3)
HER LAST FEAR (Book #4)
HER LAST CHOICE (Book #5)
HER LAST BREATH (Book #6)
HER LAST MISTAKE (Book #7)
HER LAST DESIRE (Book #8)

AVA GOLD MYSTERY SERIES
CITY OF PREY (Book #1)
CITY OF FEAR (Book #2)
CITY OF BONES (Book #3)
CITY OF GHOSTS (Book #4)
CITY OF DEATH (Book #5)
CITY OF VICE (Book #6)

A YEAR IN EUROPE
A MURDER IN PARIS (Book #1)
DEATH IN FLORENCE (Book #2)
VENGEANCE IN VIENNA (Book #3)
A FATALITY IN SPAIN (Book #4)

ELLA DARK FBI SUSPENSE THRILLER
GIRL, ALONE (Book #1)
GIRL, TAKEN (Book #2)
GIRL, HUNTED (Book #3)
GIRL, SILENCED (Book #4)
GIRL, VANISHED (Book 5)
GIRL ERASED (Book #6)
GIRL, FORSAKEN (Book #7)
GIRL, TRAPPED (Book #8)
GIRL, EXPENDABLE (Book #9)
GIRL, ESCAPED (Book #10)
GIRL, HIS (Book #11)

GIRL, LURED (Book #12)
GIRL, MISSING (Book #13)
GIRL, UNKNOWN (Book #14)

LAURA FROST FBI SUSPENSE THRILLER
ALREADY GONE (Book #1)
ALREADY SEEN (Book #2)
ALREADY TRAPPED (Book #3)
ALREADY MISSING (Book #4)
ALREADY DEAD (Book #5)
ALREADY TAKEN (Book #6)
ALREADY CHOSEN (Book #7)
ALREADY LOST (Book #8)
ALREADY HIS (Book #9)

EUROPEAN VOYAGE COZY MYSTERY SERIES
MURDER (AND BAKLAVA) (Book #1)
DEATH (AND APPLE STRUDEL) (Book #2)
CRIME (AND LAGER) (Book #3)
MISFORTUNE (AND GOUDA) (Book #4)
CALAMITY (AND A DANISH) (Book #5)
MAYHEM (AND HERRING) (Book #6)

ADELE SHARP MYSTERY SERIES
LEFT TO DIE (Book #1)
LEFT TO RUN (Book #2)
LEFT TO HIDE (Book #3)
LEFT TO KILL (Book #4)
LEFT TO MURDER (Book #5)
LEFT TO ENVY (Book #6)
LEFT TO LAPSE (Book #7)
LEFT TO VANISH (Book #8)
LEFT TO HUNT (Book #9)
LEFT TO FEAR (Book #10)
LEFT TO PREY (Book #11)
LEFT TO LURE (Book #12)
LEFT TO CRAVE (Book #13)
LEFT TO LOATHE (Book #14)
LEFT TO HARM (Book #15)

THE AU PAIR SERIES

ALMOST GONE (Book#1)
ALMOST LOST (Book #2)
ALMOST DEAD (Book #3)

ZOE PRIME MYSTERY SERIES
FACE OF DEATH (Book#1)
FACE OF MURDER (Book #2)
FACE OF FEAR (Book #3)
FACE OF MADNESS (Book #4)
FACE OF FURY (Book #5)
FACE OF DARKNESS (Book #6)

A JESSIE HUNT PSYCHOLOGICAL SUSPENSE SERIES
THE PERFECT WIFE (Book #1)
THE PERFECT BLOCK (Book #2)
THE PERFECT HOUSE (Book #3)
THE PERFECT SMILE (Book #4)
THE PERFECT LIE (Book #5)
THE PERFECT LOOK (Book #6)
THE PERFECT AFFAIR (Book #7)
THE PERFECT ALIBI (Book #8)
THE PERFECT NEIGHBOR (Book #9)
THE PERFECT DISGUISE (Book #10)
THE PERFECT SECRET (Book #11)
THE PERFECT FAÇADE (Book #12)
THE PERFECT IMPRESSION (Book #13)
THE PERFECT DECEIT (Book #14)
THE PERFECT MISTRESS (Book #15)
THE PERFECT IMAGE (Book #16)
THE PERFECT VEIL (Book #17)
THE PERFECT INDISCRETION (Book #18)
THE PERFECT RUMOR (Book #19)
THE PERFECT COUPLE (Book #20)
THE PERFECT MURDER (Book #21)
THE PERFECT HUSBAND (Book #22)
THE PERFECT SCANDAL (Book #23)
THE PERFECT MASK (Book #24)

CHLOE FINE PSYCHOLOGICAL SUSPENSE SERIES
NEXT DOOR (Book #1)

A NEIGHBOR'S LIE (Book #2)
CUL DE SAC (Book #3)
SILENT NEIGHBOR (Book #4)
HOMECOMING (Book #5)
TINTED WINDOWS (Book #6)

KATE WISE MYSTERY SERIES
IF SHE KNEW (Book #1)
IF SHE SAW (Book #2)
IF SHE RAN (Book #3)
IF SHE HID (Book #4)
IF SHE FLED (Book #5)
IF SHE FEARED (Book #6)
IF SHE HEARD (Book #7)

THE MAKING OF RILEY PAIGE SERIES
WATCHING (Book #1)
WAITING (Book #2)
LURING (Book #3)
TAKING (Book #4)
STALKING (Book #5)
KILLING (Book #6)

RILEY PAIGE MYSTERY SERIES
ONCE GONE (Book #1)
ONCE TAKEN (Book #2)
ONCE CRAVED (Book #3)
ONCE LURED (Book #4)
ONCE HUNTED (Book #5)
ONCE PINED (Book #6)
ONCE FORSAKEN (Book #7)
ONCE COLD (Book #8)
ONCE STALKED (Book #9)
ONCE LOST (Book #10)
ONCE BURIED (Book #11)
ONCE BOUND (Book #12)
ONCE TRAPPED (Book #13)
ONCE DORMANT (Book #14)
ONCE SHUNNED (Book #15)
ONCE MISSED (Book #16)
ONCE CHOSEN (Book #17)

CHAPTER ONE

Dakota woke up with a start, unsure how long she had been sleeping. She had no memory of falling asleep, or even going home –

And she wasn't home. As she blinked her eyes to try and clear them, to no success, she knew that she wasn't in a familiar place. Where was she? How did she get here?

There was something hard under her shoulder and back – a cold floor, maybe concrete or wood. She managed to turn her head, heavy and pounding, to the side enough to blink her eyes at it. Concrete. She was laying on concrete.

The room was dim, hard to see. Or maybe it was her eyes. She couldn't tell, but it felt like there was a film over them, or gauze, or a piece of dust right in her eyelashes that she couldn't blink away. Dakota tried to move again and her head spun like she was drunk. She didn't remember drinking. She felt like she might have remembered at least going to a bar, but there was nothing. Reaching for the last thing she remembered, she found it hazy and unclear. It was so hard to think. Why couldn't she think?

Things were starting to come back into focus a little the more she blinked. She groaned quietly, unable to stop as her head throbbed. She rested back against the concrete for a moment, feeling the chill spread through her skull. It was a grounding sensation, almost helpful. She was starting to see things more clearly.

The room she was in was larger than she'd thought at first. From this angle all she could really make out was a far wall with a boarded-up window, chinks of light breaking through it in a couple of spots and almost blinding her. Those rays of light played across a floor that was scattered with dead leaves and broken furniture pieces, and dust floated thickly through them. Abandoned. Wherever she was, the place was abandoned.

Music started to play somewhere behind her, making her jump mentally more than physically. When she tried to move to turn and see where the sound was coming from, she realized that it wasn't just her head holding her back from moving. She was tied up, ropes around her wrists and ankles, keeping her tightly held. She could feel them now that she was aware of them, like each small part of her body was taking its own time in coming back to her.

There was an awful taste in her mouth. Her tongue felt heavy, cottony. What had happened? Had she been drugged? Was that why she couldn't remember a thing?

Who would do that kind of thing and bring her here?

And why?

A dread rising up in her suggested that she didn't really want to know the answer.

The music was coiling around her like tendrils, an old, fuzzy kind of song that must have been from the 1930s or so. She vaguely felt she might recognize it, maybe from some old film that she'd seen. She shuffled herself, pushing her shoulder against the ground and straining against the pain in her head, until she could tilt her chin up at a more extreme angle and try to see what was happening on the other side of the room.

She caught sight of a large machine – a gramophone, her head supplied, though she didn't think she'd ever actually seen one in real life. The huge golden horn above the record player gleamed faintly in the light, and she recognized it as the source of the music. It looked old, like it was a real period gramophone that had been restored, not a replica. It must have been worth a fortune, especially given that it worked. What was it doing in an old, abandoned building like this?

Something moved in the shadows at the edges of her vision and she snapped her head round further, reeling from the way her brain seemed to rock against her skull, until she saw it fully. A shape. No – a man. He was standing not far from the gramophone, watching her. Doing something. Tying something – a bowtie. He was tying a bowtie around his neck.

Why was he tying a bowtie around his neck?

Everything seemed incongruous, impossible to explain. A man tying a bowtie, an ancient gramophone playing an old song, an abandoned building. And what was her place among all of them? Why was she here?

The man began to move towards her, and shafts of light fell over him as he walked through them, illuminating his face before plunging it back into shadow. She didn't recognize him. If you found yourself tied up in an abandoned building listening to gramophone music, there was a certain expectation, she felt, that you would see someone you knew. A best friend who would shout 'surprise' before the rest of the party

2

appeared. A sorority sister to explain that this was all part of Hell Week. She had no idea what other context there could be, what other reason she could have for being here.

Maybe she'd fainted and they'd tied her up to stop her having a fit and brought her to the nearest shelter while they waited for an ambulance –

But she knew, even as she sought desperately for an innocent reason, that this wasn't the case.

She'd been drugged, tied up, and brought here – to a place where no one would think to look.

That was what this was, wasn't it?

And this man, this man moving towards her…

Was he just going to kill her?

Or worse?

"May I have this dance?" he said, his voice a low murmur but strong and proud against the backdrop of the music, like he was the male lead in a movie. He stretched out a hand towards her, like she would reach up and take it, like this was prom and he was the boy she'd been crushing on all year.

She wanted to ask him who he was. Why he'd brought her here. What this was all about. What he was going to do. How he expected her to take his hand when she was tied up on the floor.

Instead, Dakota only managed a whimper.

"Of course," he said, his voice that same husky low tone, as if he was putting it on. "How silly of me. Allow me to help you up."

Dakota couldn't shrink away from him fast enough. He reached down around her knees and took her shoulders and lifted her into the air, tilting her until her feet met the floor. She was still wearing her shoes. In fact, she was fully dressed. That seemed like a good sign, didn't it? But still…

The song stopped on the record player, and there was a scratching, empty kind of noise as the record rotated alone, no music left to play. The man steadied her on her feet, almost gently, catching her when she almost toppled over and then holding her by the arms until she had her balance back. Dakota felt like she was going to be sick. Had she hit her head? Was that why she felt this way? All she knew was that something wasn't right. She was woozy, out of it, desperately trying to keep her head so she could figure out what was going on.

"Stay there," he said, which was unnecessary, because her legs were bound.

All she could manage was a tiny shuffle at most, and with her balance so badly impaired, she didn't even want to risk it.

He moved back to the gramophone and pressed something, or moved or did something – she couldn't see – and the record started over from the beginning again. It was a sultry kind of song, like they all seemed to be from that time. A woman's voice cut over the sound of the band, giving the impression of a smoky bar, a crowd of well-dressed patrons dancing and drinking together.

He was my man, and we were so happy
Two fools in love, how now it may seem

He turned and walked towards her again, and reached behind her. There was a kind of release of tension, a snap of something metallic, and she found her arms free. She reached out, trying immediately to push him away –

Something around her back snapped into place and held her wrists apart, a hard line pressing against her skin from behind, her arms not moving any further than just past her own sides. A rope. There was a rope between them, kept at a deliberate length so that she could not bring her hands together in front of her.

What was he planning to do to her?

The singer continued her breathy tune, the lyrics seeming to enfold Dakota in a haze.

Now when I think of how I was happy
I don't recall was it nightmare or dream

"There we are," he said, taking each of her hands. He stepped in close to her as though they were lovers dancing cheek to cheek, placing one of her hands on his shoulder and taking the other in his own hand. After a brief pause to wait for the next line to start, he began to move, turning around her and dragging her feet slightly in some awful parody of a dance.

She came along, with a rose in her hair
Pretty and young, with a smile like sunshine

He was so strange in his movements, almost tender with her, like they were on some dancefloor in a bar or alone in a kitchen, dancing to show their love. But she'd seen his face now and she still had no idea who he was, no clue as to why he had brought her here. No understanding of what his motive for this dance was.

That was what scared her the most – because even as tender as he was being, she knew she must be in danger.

4

The singer began to sing a new line, but Dakota never heard it – he whirled her suddenly, thrusting her at arm's length from himself, making her almost topple over. His grip on the top of her arms tightened painfully, making her catch her breath in a sob.

And then she saw his face.

He wasn't soft and gentle anymore. He wasn't a gentleman. He was looking at her with his upper lip raised in a snarl, and there was so much anger in his eyes that she flinched, trying to tear herself out of his grip.

It only occurred to her as she was falling that maybe he wanted her to throw herself to the ground, where it was even harder for her to get away.

She hit the concrete hard, going down on her elbow with no real way to catch herself, the wind knocked out of her as the impact of the ground hit her body and then her legs. She struggled to find a breath. At least it wasn't her head. She hadn't hit her head. She still had enough strength to roll over and start to crawl – gasping in pain as she realized she'd done something bad to her elbow – trying to get even an inch further away from him –

Something hard and heavy struck her from behind, and she felt something give in her chest, something wrong. A moment later as she looked down and saw bright red blood pooling on the floor below her, she felt the pain. It wasn't just pressure or a strike – something had pierced her – something pinning her to the ground –

Dakota opened her mouth to cry out in pain but the sound died on her lips, not enough breath left in her body to make it. She felt something else heavy on her back, just in one spot on her shoulder – a booted foot, pressing down on her. And then the pressure reversing, the piercing thing withdrawing from her chest and her back.

Dakota tasted something metallic in her mouth. She thought for a second about her little brother, who was waiting at home for her – was he waiting? – how long had it been? – and then nothing else, the world going black around her for good this time.

5

CHAPTER TWO

Laura blinked at the sound of Lacey's voice calling from the sofa. She must have zoned out for a moment, gone somewhere in her head.

That had been happening a lot in the last week, since she'd had that horrible vision.

"I'm just finishing up your sandwich, sweetie," Laura called back. "You want crusts or no crusts?"

"No crusts," Lacey replied immediately, twisting on the sofa to look over the side cushions and give Laura a wide-eyed look which made her mother laugh. The five-year-old hated crusts, as most children seemed to for some reason. She blinked her blue eyes at Laura's laughter and then tossed her blonde hair to look back at the show she was watching on the TV, doing her best impression of a grumpy teenager already.

Laura took the knife she'd used to slice the cheese and deftly sliced off the crusts on all four sides of Lacey's sandwich, adding them to her own plate since there was no reason to waste good food. Using the knife made her hand tremble for a moment as she put it down. Was that what Chris had been using in her vision? Was it a knife?

She took a deep breath, trying to think more clearly. It seemed like everything she did, said, saw, or heard was enough to take her back to that moment. She'd been sitting in a café with Zach, the only other psychic she'd ever met in her life, and both of them were trying to work out why their powers were acting up. She'd touched his hand to reassure him, and then she'd seen it.

Chris, her boyfriend of not too many months – if she could still call him a boyfriend at her age, since it sounded like something you said in your twenties – crouching over Zach. Plunging a hand down and stabbing him in the chest. And the way Zach looked – prone, like he was out cold, only there was a look of terrible pain and fear on his face.

It had only been a vision of a moment's length, but she hadn't been able to get it out of her head.

Laura grabbed the two plates she had prepared and carried them over to the sofa, handing one to Lacey and keeping the other on her own lap. "What are we watching?" she asked.

"This is my favorite show," Lacey declared – just one more thing to squeeze Laura's heart painfully. If she'd had full-time custody of her daughter, she would have known things like this. Only getting to see her on the weekends was tough, and she knew there was so much she was missing. After Marcus, Lacey's father, banned Laura from seeing her at all for so long, she'd already missed so much. The thought of missing a single second more was so painful to her.

Almost as painful as the thought that she'd been wrong about Christopher Fallow when she'd finally decided to trust him.

It hadn't been a thoughtless moment or a whim. She'd taken time to get to know him, to make sure he wasn't anything like his violent and abusive brother. To be sure that he was going to be a good guardian for his niece now that she had neither of her biological parents to turn to anymore. Falling for him, well, that had happened somewhere along the way, by accident.

But that was Chris. It was hard not to adore him. He was a doctor – a cardiologist – who had spent years of his life doing aid work overseas in communities that couldn't afford proper care. When his own brother had been jailed for killing his wife, he hadn't hesitated for a moment – he'd given up his charity work, come back home, and taken his niece in. He was wonderful with Amy, and even more adorable was how badly he wanted to be wonderful for her.

And yet…

What Laura had seen in that moment wasn't a kind, gentle, giving soul. It had been an act of stunning violence, perpetrated on a helpless old man.

Laura put her arm around Lacey and held her a little tighter, fervently hoping she was wrong.

Her visions had never failed her before. They were always right, one way or another. But lately… lately, things had been going in a different direction. Her visions had been unpredictable. She'd started seeing the past as well as the future. And on her last case, she'd thought she'd fulfilled the vision and caught their killer, only for the same scene to happen to her in real life, effectively twice. With all of this going on, it was hard not to hope that the vision wasn't trustworthy at all.

That maybe, somehow, Chris wasn't about to turn into a violent psychopath and kill a man that Laura had only just met – but needed badly, because he was the only one she had ever known who could provide insight into her gift.

"Are we going to see Amy today, Mommy?" Lacey asked.

Laura bit her lip. It was only natural for Lacey to assume, really. They had settled into a nice routine of going over to Chris's house on Saturdays so the girls could have a playdate. This week, though, Laura hadn't confirmed with Chris. Instead, she'd made up an excuse about appointments and put him off. When they hadn't gone around yesterday, Lacey must have thought they would be going today, Sunday, instead.

"Not this time, sweetie," Laura said. "I thought we could have a Mommy and Lacey day, just the two of us. What do you think?"

Lacey pouted slightly.

"And some ice cream?" Laura added, knowing it was a bribe but preferring to keep her daughter happy than to think about that too much.

"Okay," Lacey chirped happily, swinging her legs against the sofa seat as she turned her attention back to the screen.

Laura hugged her again, pressing a kiss to the top of her head. Lacey endured it rather than responding, keeping her focus on the screen and then giggling at the antics of one of the cartoon characters.

Laura sighed quietly to herself, taking a bite of her neglected sandwich. She'd had to field three requests to meet from Chris and one from Zach already, and it had only been a week. She was starting to run out of valid-sounding excuses for why she couldn't see them. But the more she kept them apart, the less likely it was that either of them would be in danger – and the less she saw of them, the less likely it was that she would get hurt so much when her vision came true.

Which was nonsense, of course. She was going to hurt if it came true. She was going to hurt badly. She had invested so much in the idea of Chris, and Zach was the help she had been waiting on for decades.

How was she going to cope if she lost both of them in the same moment?

Her eyes strayed to the drawer in the kitchen where she used to keep bottles of wine, and she knew what the answer was. She would cope the only way she knew how, if she wasn't strong enough to resist. For Lacey's sake, she'd been sober for a long time now. Longer than she'd ever managed it before. She had to keep it up.

If she didn't, she'd lose Lacey again. And that couldn't happen. Losing all three of them one after the other – no, she wouldn't be able to cope with that in any universe, under any circumstances.

Laura hugged Lacey tighter again.

"Mommy," Lacey said, squirming. "I'm watching my show."

8

"Oh, sorry." Laura consciously loosened her grip. "Don't forget your sandwich."

It was probably a good thing, for Lacey's sake, that Laura's cell phone started to ring on the coffee table. As she reached for it, she thought maybe she was about to get a distraction that would help her to stop obsessing over the vision.

Then she saw Zach's name on the caller ID, and she knew it was only about to get worse.

"Hello?" Laura said into the phone, holding it to her ear as she got up from the sofa and left Lacey with her cartoons.

"Laura, it's Zach," he said, as if he didn't realize that she had caller ID. "I just had the most interesting vision."

"Oh?" Laura asked, feeling her heart sink into her feet. She was going to be sick. She turned and leaned against the kitchen sink, thinking at least she would be able to splash water on her face if she needed it.

"You were walking down the street, and then you turned to go into this house," Zach said. "A very nice house, actually. Really big. You know, one of those ones in the east suburbs, I think."

Laura's mouth went dry. Chris's house. He had to be describing Chris's house. "I was?" she asked, feeling like a puppet in a show, reciting the lines Zach expected of her without much feeling.

"Yes, and you were with a handsome man," Zach continued. "Very handsome, sort of a next door type but with that look that wealthy people have, you know? Well-groomed, well-dressed, and so on. And there were two little girls running into the house ahead of you."

Chris and Amy and Lacey. "I see," Laura said.

"Well?" Zach prompted. "Does it remind you of anyone?"

"You know I have a daughter," Laura said. She turned to glance at Lacey, but the little girl was focused on the TV, not paying attention to her Mommy's phone call at all. "We have playdates sometimes at a friend's house."

"He looked like more than a friend," Zach said, sounding every bit the jolly grandad trying to ask his grandchild whether they had their first boy- or girlfriend.

"Yes, we're seeing each other," Laura admitted, because it was pointless not to. "Did anything happen in this vision, or was that it?" She felt a pit in her stomach at what he might have been about to say, but she had to know. Surely, if he was calling her to say he'd seen his own death, he wouldn't sound so cheerful. It made her feel even sicker

9

all the same. If he had seen it too, there would be no denying it – no way to justify seeing Chris again, knowing...

"That was all," Zach said. "Strange, isn't it? I think I'm supposed to meet this chap of yours."

"What?" Laura said, glancing over to Lacey to make sure her sharply raised voice hadn't disturbed her. "No, I don't think you should do that."

"Why not?"

"He doesn't know," Laura said, keeping her words carefully chosen just in case Lacey was listening after all. "I wouldn't be able to explain to him who you are."

"Well, that's alright," Zach said. "We can come up with a cover story. Maybe I'm a distant uncle of yours."

"I don't want to lie to him," Laura said.

"A work colleague, then," Zach insisted. "That wouldn't be a lie – not really. We're both gifted with the same set of skills. Or perhaps you could imply you know me from AA without actually saying it."

Laura shook her head even though he couldn't see her, pinching the bridge of her nose. This wasn't happening. She was trying so hard to keep them apart, and now... "Look, you can't meet him because no one's allowed to know we're together," she lied, scrambling to find anything that might make him stop trying. "If you walk up to us in the street I'd have to pretend I don't know Chris or that I'm just babysitting or something. It would be awkward and horrible. And he'd probably get upset and insist that we never go out in public again, so please don't ruin things for me."

Laura felt a little bad about trashing Chris's reputation like this. It was all made up, of course. She'd visited Chris at work, so she was pretty sure anyone on his team would know about them, and they weren't shy about going out together. But it was the only thing she could think of, other than the truth.

And there was no way she was telling the truth. If Zach knew that Chris was destined to kill him, there was no telling what he might do. The old man might even be stupid enough to seek Chris out on purpose.

"Hmm, well," Zach said. "I hope you don't think I'm intruding, but I do think a young woman like yourself should find a man who is proud to be with them."

Laura bit back a response. If there was one thing she'd figured out about Zach so far, it was that he wanted to help people. It was why he had dedicated his life to being a teacher. He had a natural kind of grandfatherly instinct. It was sweet, even if she didn't want the advice. Even if, in this case, the advice was meaningless because it didn't reflect her situation at all.

"I have to go," she said hastily. Her phone had started to buzz again, a call coming through on a different line, an excellent excuse to stop talking with Zach. The excuse she needed. She even wished she'd thought of it earlier. "I'll talk to you later."

She had no real desire to talk to him again later, as it happened – she was hoping that he would wait for her call for so long that he would forget to call back himself. That way, she wouldn't have to keep making up lies to appease him. Until she figured all this out and could call him herself, she wanted to avoid any risks.

She accepted the other call and put the phone back to her ear – knowing, this time, who to expect. It was Division Chief Rondelle, her direct superior in the FBI – and the fact that he was calling her on the weekend was only an indication of one possible thing.

"Chief," she said, by way of greeting.

"Agent Frost," he said, which meant he was definitely in work mode. He occasionally would call her Laura, but only really when their conversations took on a more personal tone – or when he needed to beg her to stop causing trouble. "We've got a new case I'd like you to take. Please come in for briefing as quickly as you can."

"Wait," Laura said. She paused, trying to think. "Where is it? Do we need to go now?"

"It's a short journey, right over the D.C. border in Maryland," Rondelle explained. "The opposite direction from your last case, but you're still in luck with how close it is. And yes, now would be good. It seems like time is of the essence with this one. As it is with them all, really."

Laura bit her lip, thinking. That was good luck. She would be close enough by that she could rush back if someone needed her at home – if there was something wrong with Lacey, or if Chris and Zach did end up meeting after all. Not that there would be a lot she could do about it after the fact, if Zach was dead.

But on the other hand, she'd be far enough away and busy enough that she could easily make excuses about not being able to see either of them. Maybe she'd be even luckier and this would be a long case, one that kept her away all week. She wouldn't want it to take much longer and keep her away from Lacey, but a whole week without making things up to put them off…

11

"Sure," Laura said, even though he hadn't told her anything about it yet, because it was a good enough reason to get out of the sticky situation she was in and she wasn't about to look a gift horse in the mouth. "I'll be there. I just... I have Lacey, so I have to get her home to her father first. Can you give me an extra half hour?"

"I can," Rondelle said, though he sounded grudging with it. "Get her back safe. Don't speed."

"I won't," Laura said, half a smile in her voice because Rondelle pretended to be so gruff but, underneath it all, he was clearly a softie, really. She hung up, turning back to the sofa to tell Lacey to get ready.

But Lacey was not on the sofa. She was standing near Laura in the kitchen, with her hands on her hips, a sulky look on her five-year-old face.

"You said we were going to get ice cream," she said, her tone accusatory.

"We are, baby," Laura said, already starting to reach for things. Her keys on the counter. Marcus' number in her phone book so she could let him know she was on the way back. She tried not to feel her heart throbbing painfully in her chest at the thought she was letting Lacey down. Parents had to prioritize work sometimes – that was a common thing. Especially as an FBI agent, her family had to accept that she sometimes had to go into work at odd times.

This had been the best solution to all of her problems – so why did it feel like she was the worst mother in the world?

"I heard you," Lacey said, stomping her foot. "You're going to work and I've got to go back to Daddy."

"And we can get ice cream on the way," Laura said, grateful that Rondelle had said that last line about driving slowly – maybe she could pretend it really took her that long to get there if she fitted in an ice cream break. Lacey probably didn't realize it, but right at that moment, she could have asked for a pony – and Laura would have stopped to get her one of those along the way, too. Anything to try to make it up to her. "Now, go on, let's get your stuff."

Laura mentally checked off all the things she needed to do before arriving at HQ, and how long it was going to take, as Lacey traipsed off to find her bag in her room. It was a good thing that, knowing today was the day Lacey needed to go back home anyway, Laura had helped her pack away most of her things this morning.

Right now, Laura thought, there was so much going on in her head that for once, she was actually looking forward to taking on a case –

especially knowing she'd be able to lean on her partner, Nate, while they were out there.

CHAPTER THREE

Laura strode down the corridor towards Nate, nodding at him as she did. He pushed away from the wall he'd been leaning on and stood up straight, rubbing a hand over his close-cropped black hair as he waited for her to catch up. He looked like he might have been waiting for a while.

"Hey," he said, his voice low as she approached.

"Sorry," Laura replied. "I had to get Lacey back to Marcus."

Nate shook his head. "I get it. To be honest, I thought you might tell Rondelle you didn't want the case."

"And let you be partnered with some rookie instead?" Laura flashed him a wan smile. "I've done that enough lately to not want to put anyone else through it."

Nate's returned smile was equally weak. It was still a little bit of an awkward topic – the time Nate had spent away from her after he declared he wanted to transfer and not be her partner anymore. At first it was because she wouldn't tell him her secret – and then when she caved and told him about her psychic powers, she thought she'd lost him for good. Having him back now meant the world, and Laura wished she hadn't said anything – she didn't want to jeopardize things now they were back on relatively stable ground.

"Shall we head in?" Nate suggested, which was an absolute relief. Laura nodded, letting him go first to knock on Division Chief Rondelle's door.

"Come in," he shouted from inside, and they did as they were told.

Rondelle was behind his desk as always – Laura often thought that it was entirely possible he'd been fused in place, it was so unusual to see him anywhere else. Or maybe he'd been chained to the room somehow by invisible bonds. Whatever it was, she'd yet to find a time of day or night when the older man, with his graying hair and shorter stature, wasn't in his office.

"Good to see you've decided to stop gossiping in the corridor and come in," Rondelle said, and Laura took a breath. Clearly, the Chief was in a bad mood. "I've got your briefing here." He tossed a folder towards the far end of his desk rather than waiting for one of them to come and take it from his hand, going back to whatever paperwork he was working on immediately.

"Is there anything we need to know?" Nate asked hesitantly, sharing a sideways glance with Laura. She tried to subtly signal to him not to poke the bear, but it was too late. Rondelle looked up with a frustrated sigh.

"Read it yourself," he said. "You've got a nice drive ahead of you and you both have eyes, ears, and mouths. One of you can read it out loud to the other. Go on – you've already wasted enough time."

Laura didn't need to be told twice – she made a beeline for the door before Rondelle could start yelling.

She wanted to say something to Nate badly, but remembering Rondelle's comment about gossiping in the corridor and realizing he must have heard them talking before, she held her tongue all the way down to the elevator. Only once the doors slid shut did she turn to Nate with wide eyes and let it out.

"What was going on with him?" she asked, shaking her head.

"I don't know," Nate frowned. "Sounded bad, though. Maybe he's just sore about having to work on a Sunday."

Laura snorted. "As if he doesn't work every Sunday."

"Who's driving?" Nate asked, after flashing her a grin in response that seemed more genuine this time.

"You can," Laura said, stifling a yawn. "I've had a busy weekend. What are we doing when we get there? Meeting the locals or going to the motel?"

Nate shrugged. "He didn't say. Is there anything in the briefing?"

Laura flipped through the meagre pages quickly, scanning them. "Nope," she said, trying to ignore the glimpse of the crime scene photographs. They could wait their turn.

"Then I guess it's up to us," Nate said.

"I say we get some sleep and get over to the local precinct first thing," Laura said decisively. "By the time we've driven over there, it'll be late evening, and it's a long drive too. A lot of concentration. We're no good when we're exhausted."

Nate gave her an odd look as they stepped out of the elevator and into the reception, walking straight out across it towards the parking lot entrance. "You normally want to hit the ground running."

It was true. In almost all other cases, Laura was keen to get the case done as quickly as possible and get back home. She always wanted to be there for Lacey, or make sure she didn't miss a date with Chris, or keep up with other commitments. But this time – this time she almost wished the case would take as long as possible. Maybe the killer was done and he'd go to ground, one of those impossible cases where no new clues ever came in and you just had to hope one day technology would advance, after spending months trying to solve it in the first place.

So long as no one else died, Laura was quite happy for this case to take forever. And there was nothing she could say to Nate that wouldn't cause more problems than having his listening ear would solve.

She shrugged, pretending to be casual. "Just being pragmatic," she said. "We'll work better in the morning than we would tonight after a long drive."

"Fair enough," Nate said, pushing open the doors ahead of her and walking to his car.

They got in quickly, Laura diverting for just a moment to her own car to grab her bug-out bag, which she always kept ready for travel. She took a moment's breath as she hesitated at the back of her vehicle, pretending it was taking her longer than it really was. She needed that moment to gather herself. To try to put the vision out of her head.

She couldn't stand to tell Nate. Even though he was the only one other than Zach who knew about her visions, she couldn't open up to him about this one. What would he think? What would he want to do? You couldn't arrest someone based on a psychic vision of something they might do in the future.

All Laura could do now was try to stop it from happening by keeping them apart. But if Nate knew that she knew, and she just went on living her life and seeing Chris and letting him see Lacey, what would he think of her?

Laura tried not to let her mind stray to how she felt about herself right then, locking her car and walking back towards Nate with a more casual expression wallpapered carefully onto her face.

With the trunk packed, Nate started the engine and set out, and Laura settled into the passenger seat with the file in her hand.

"Alright," she said, opening it back up to the first page, glad of the distraction. "What have we got... looks like two deaths so far, both women."

"So far, so normal," Nate joked. It was true. You didn't normally call the FBI on an urgent case for just one murder. Just one murder was something you admitted you needed help with after a week or so. It was when you had all the hallmarks of a serial killer or a spree killer that you called urgently – and two very similar killings that weren't apparently gang-related definitely fit that bill.

"The report says they were both taken or abducted and then killed in a different location," Laura said. "Looks like our first victim was reportedly on her way home but never arrived, and then was found in an abandoned apartment building that was scheduled for demolition. Then, our second victim was thought to be at home and probably only stepped outside to run an errand, and wasn't reported missing during the day. They only knew she'd gone when she was found later that day in an empty store that had been cleared out and left boarded up for a few years."

"Great," Nate sighed. "So let's just put better barriers around all the abandoned buildings in this town and leave the locals to sort it out. They'll get him eventually when he trips some motion-activated surveillance."

Laura cast him a glance as they pulled out of the parking lot and onto the road. "Something got into you, too?"

"Sorry," Nate sighed. "I think Chief Rondelle is rubbing off on me. That, and it would be nice to just get a damn Sunday night to myself without having to head off on a case."

"You could have turned it down," Laura pointed out.

"And leave you to work with a rookie?" Nate replied, using her own words back at her. He sighed and shook his head. "No, it's fine. Part of the territory, right?"

Laura narrowed her eyes at him. "Did you have a date tonight?"

Nate paused, chuckled, and rubbed the back of his neck. "Guilty."

Laura laughed, shaking her head. She knew what it was like to have to put your personal life on hold for the job – after all, she'd done the same thing herself so many times.

"Anyway," she said, moving back to the briefing notes, as Nate settled into a comfortable driving pace along the road. "This is a little more unusual: at each of the scenes, they've found a gramophone set up near the body."

"A gramophone?" Nate frowned. "That's a new one on me. What is he doing, using it to crush them to death?"

"No, looks like they're stabbed," Laura said. "With lethal precision, actually. It says here they bled out within a matter of minutes – consciousness would be lost in more like seconds. Nothing on the murder weapon here, so I'm guessing they don't yet know what it is – just a blade."

"Swords and gramophones," Nate grunted. "Yep, sounds like a weird one alright. Anything connecting the two victims?"

"Not at first glance," Laura said, running her eyes over their stats. "But we'll know more when we get there."

"That we will," Nate agreed, turning onto the highway that would take them out of the city.

CHAPTER FOUR

Nate drummed his fingers on the steering wheel as they waited at a light, glancing up at the rearview mirror to check who was behind before looking to the side slyly. Laura was staring out of the passenger side window, probably not even aware that he had looked in her direction.

Nate held back a sigh and looked forward again, keeping his eyes on the lights and waiting for them to change.

"I think we're close," he said, something that wouldn't normally be necessary. Usually, Laura was switched on enough to be watching the GPS, aware of how close they were. Usually, she would be chomping at the bit to get out and start investigating.

"Okay," Laura said, without much enthusiasm, resuming her silent stare at the passing scenery.

Nate bit his tongue, trying hard not to say anything. He was trying to respect her privacy, especially since she'd come clean and actually told him about her gift. He was trying to trust her.

It was just hard when he knew for a fact she was holding something back.

But whatever it was, whatever was bothering her and had her lost in thought for most of their journey, she didn't want to say it. Not yet. Nate knew it was best for him to wait, to see if she would say it herself, instead of pushing. He kept quiet, following the GPS and turning right into the motel parking lot.

"Here we are," Nate said, trying to prompt Laura's attention to actually look around. She finally stirred, glancing up at the complex – same as always: a few stories of plain-looking rooms ranged along balconies, a parking lot, and a small shelter near the entrance where a bored attendant was waiting for people to check in.

"I'll go get the keys," she said. Nate paused the car near the entrance to the lot for her to get out, then drove on to park.

If she didn't snap out of this by the morning, he was maybe going to have to say something – even if he knew that it could potentially set them at odds. Because if she wasn't prepared to pay any attention to the investigation with how distracted she was, it was going to be his duty to intervene. Friends or not, they were also colleagues – and they had one of the most important jobs in the world.

Saving lives.

***

Nate looked up and blinked in the early morning sun as Laura rushed to the passenger side door, throwing herself into the seat and nodding at him to go. He started the engine while carefully running over her appearance in his mind. She looked like normal Laura. Blonde hair up in a smooth ponytail, sharp black suit like they all wore, determination on her face. Not as distracted as she had been last night.

He hoped that was going to be the end of it – but he had a feeling whatever it was that had been playing on her mind hadn't been resolved that easily.

"Straight to the most recent scene?" Nate suggested.

Laura nodded smartly. "Might as well hit the ground running," she said. She seemed sharper this morning, at least. Nate pulled out of the parking lot and turned in the direction of the rising sun. He'd already set the GPS up and called ahead. He'd been worried enough about Laura to actually beat her out of his room this morning.

"It's not far," Nate said. "Should only be five minutes."

"Any updates overnight?"

Nate shook his head. "Nothing they've passed on to me. Guess we'll have to see. We should be meeting the captain in charge of the investigation there."

Laura nodded, pulling the file from the dashboard and going over the pages again. Nate got the feeling she hadn't taken in all the information she wanted to last night. At least she was recognizing and rectifying that.

Nate followed the GPS for the short route until they came up to a spot that was clearly the right one: several marked police cars were parked around a boarded-up store, still with the old, faded signs visible above the door. Nate parked nearby as best as he could, which was a little bit of a challenge given the number of official vehicles – and the couple of local news vans which had joined them. A bored-looking reporter jumped to her feet when she saw Nate and Laura get out of their car, but Nate led the way fast and ducked under crime tape, reaching the door, and flashing his badge at the detective there. They

20

were inside before she had a chance to get her cameraman in position, which was a relief.

Though he knew the news crews would still be out there when they left.

"Captain?" he called out experimentally, glancing around inside the space they had entered. It was a large enough store, which was perhaps why it had been difficult to find a new owner – it would have cost a fair amount to buy or lease, and the location seemed to be more on the outskirts of town. Not a compelling prospect for most businesses.

It was also fairly dark inside, save for some spotlights that had been set up at one end of the store – leaving the rest of it even harder to see, given the contrast.

"Ah, agents!" someone called back. Nate deduced the voice was coming from somewhere behind the lights, and followed Laura as she led the way towards it. He figured she must have been able to see better than he could, so he let her take charge.

"Captain…?" Laura greeted him. She held out a hand to shake for the man who did eventually emerge from the gloom: he was dark-haired, tall, and tan, and younger than most captains. If anything, he looked like a politician, which put Nate's back up immediately.

"Captain Kinnock," he said, turning to shake Nate's hand next. His handshake was firm and direct, applying just a little too much pressure. Nate was unperturbed, deliberately increasing the pressure from his side to match and then raise it. Kinnock let go and dropped his hand by his side as if he wanted to shake it a little but resisted.

Nate wanted to smirk, but he also resisted.

"Special Agent Laura Frost, and my partner Special Agent Nathaniel Lavoie," Laura said. She always liked to get the introductions and small talk out of the way as quickly as possible so that they could get down to the actual work. "This is the second crime scene?"

"Yes," Kinnock confirmed, turning towards the area illuminated by the lights. Even though dawn was breaking outside, the boarded-up windows wouldn't let any light in. "This is where she was found. And here, the gramophone."

Laura scanned the area quickly. Nate could almost see her brain working. He felt a small flare of excitement: Was she going to get a vision here? The last case had been almost disappointing. He wanted to see what her abilities could really do. He'd been waiting long enough – maybe this time she would really see something that would help.

"Has everything been forensically checked? Including the area outside of the light?" Laura asked.

"Of course," Kinnock said, looking a bit affronted if anything. "We covered the whole area yesterday during the day. This is all that's left. The body is already in the morgue."

"The gramophone," Laura said. "Are the models the same at both crime scenes?"

"Yes, they're the same," Kinnock replied. "Same record loaded onto both of them, too."

That had Laura raising her eyebrows. Nate felt the same way. "What's the record?" he asked, wandering over towards the gramophone. He carefully skirted a large dark stain on the floor – clearly the blood lost by the victim. Judging by the size of the stain, she'd lost a lot.

"I haven't heard of it before this case," Kinnock admitted. "Research tells us it's from the 1930s. It's called *My Man and the Rose*, by this singer called Nena Flora. Either of you know it?"

Nate shook his head. "Never heard of the singer, either," he said.

Laura had followed him, and she bent, trying to figure out how to make the device work. "Does it play?" she asked.

Nate reached over and turned the crank on the side, checking the needle was settled on the record in the right place and then standing back. It only took a moment for the sound of the song to fill the room around them. It was a slow, sultry kind of tune, just right for a slow dance, and the gramophone produced it beautifully. It was like the pair were meant for each other. This kind of song played on a modern device just wouldn't have felt right.

He was my man, and we were so happy
Two fools in love, how now it may seem
Now when I think of how I was happy
I don't recall was it nightmare or dream

Laura stirred a little, as if breaking out from a spell that the song was trying to put them under. Nate got the feeling. It was a voice from a distinct past, the crackle and noise of the age layered over the voice that must have been clear as day in real life. Coupled with the dusty, abandoned store and this cleared space at one end of it, it made him feel like he was time traveling.

"I don't know it," she said. "It sounds like a lot of those old songs to me."

Nate nodded agreement. "Definitely a product of its time, that kind of style back then," he said.

"Did you get anything from the forensic sweep?" Laura asked, turning back to look over at Kinnock. The song carried on playing, eerie and slow, raising goosebumps on Nate's arms.

Kinnock shook his head. "We have some partial prints, but none of them are matched to anything on our database. It's the same with the last scene. They could only be found on the gramophone itself."

"Interesting," Laura said. "So, it's possible our killer has no criminal record to date."

"Or that he bought the gramophones from the same place, where a particular member of the staff handled them," Nate suggested, just to make sure they were considering all theories.

"Hmm." Laura was clearly unhappy with the premise. He had to agree – it was always a shame when you got no forensic lead at all. Fingerprints could be worked with. All they had to do was find a viable suspect, take his prints, and boom – the case could be solved, just like that. But if they turned out to be a red herring, it could set them back a long way. As always with the kind of cases they took on, everything had to be approached with caution.

"We should move on," Nate suggested. The song was still playing, and – though he didn't want to admit it – it was creepy as hell. Hearing it in this space, the way the woman's sad and aching voice seemed to caress all those cobwebbed shelves and boarded windows, felt like being in a horror movie. And he didn't want to be there for the jump scare.

"Good idea," Laura said, turning to Kinnock. She wouldn't say it either, but he was sure she felt it, too. There was enough creepiness in murders like this in the first place, without adding more. "I'd like to speak to whoever found the body."

"He's right outside," Kinnock said, gesturing for them to walk with him.

"Oh?" Nate frowned, thinking back. "I didn't see anyone out there but one of your cops."

"That's right," Kinnock nodded. "It was him who found it."

Laura frowned as well, looking back at Kinnock over her shoulder as they reached the door. "This wasn't found by a member of the public and then called in?"

"Well," Kinnock said, and then hesitated. "You know, I think it's better if you hear it directly from Officer Munson."

With a mysterious hint like that, Nate was beginning to think this case was turning out to be a lot more complex than it first seemed. He reached for the door, ready to get outside and find out just what was going on here.

CHAPTER FIVE

Laura stepped out into a morning that was a lot more established than the one they had left behind, the sun stretching its fingers over the neighborhood. It was a lot easier to see, now, that this whole area was in decline. It wasn't just the store that was abandoned. A couple of homes across the way looked like they might be, too.

"Officer Munson?" she guessed, turning to the cop who had been guarding the door when they went inside. He stood at attention and nodded sharply. "You found the body?"

"Yes, ma'am," he said, then hesitated. He was a younger officer, green-eyed and dark-haired, which was unusual in itself. She was beginning to feel like there was a spell over this whole case, enchanting things to make them look and sound far more romantic than they really were. "Well, kind of. I was tipped off."

"Explain," Laura said, crossing her arms over her chest. She didn't mean it to come across as harsh or rude, but she needed to get at the facts. In her experience, time spent on trying to be polite and make small talk would be better spent on actually investigating the case.

"Well," Munson said, shifting his stance self-consciously. "I was waiting on a call-out from dispatch at the station. The phone at my desk rang so I answered it, and there was a man on the other end of the line. He said there was a body that was sitting in this property and that we had to get there fast."

"What did you say?" Laura asked. There was something here, something tugging at the edges of her mind. You didn't just make a call directly to an officer's desk if you were a bystander who'd found a body. You called 911.

"I asked him to repeat it," Munson said. "I was confused, you know? Like, why did we need to get there fast? Was there a chance that the victim was going to make it? Maybe did they think that the killer was still around and we could catch them red-handed? And the guy's voice was so calm, you know. Like, nothing was happening. Just cool as anything."

"He didn't sound distressed or surprised at all?" Laura asked.

"He sounded like he was ordering a pizza," Munson said bluntly. He shook his head, looking down at the ground for a moment. "Anyway, when I asked him to repeat it, he got real upset with me. Started yelling. He said, 'didn't you hear me? I said you need to get there now!' Like, he yelled it down the line, you know? It was this quick shift, zero to sixty. Then he put the phone down."

"That doesn't sound like a bystander," Laura said, voicing her thoughts to Nate. "That's a killer who wanted to get you to the crime scene at a certain time."

Nate nodded. "Is there a recording of the call we can hear for ourselves?"

Munson, shook his head, his fingers flexing as he hooked them into his belt. "Sorry. If it came in through dispatch we'd have it recorded, but it was on my own direct line."

"Who would have known you were at your desk?" Laura asked.

Munson shook his head. "I don't know. But I'm near a window. Anyone could have seen me from outside, I guess."

Laura sighed. That would complicate things. For just a moment, she'd been hopeful that they had an inside job. Someone who knew which cops were on duty, which were in the office, and could target the one they wanted. No such luck.

"What did you find when you got here?" Nate asked.

"Well, we screamed over here in the car as quick as we could, me and my partner," Munson said. "He went around the back to check out the surrounding area and see if anyone was trying to escape, and I went inside. That's when I heard it. The song. And I knew it was just like the other one."

Laura exchanged a glance with Nate. "The music was actually playing when you got there?" she said.

"Yeah," Munson confirmed. "Creepy as all hell. And the woman was lying there on the floor in front of it. She had her wrists and ankles still bound and there was a pool of blood right around her. I knew she was dead soon as I looked at her."

Laura turned to Nate again. "The song was still playing," she said. Inside the store, the music had stopped. "How long was that record, do you think? Three minutes? Four?"

"Something like that," Nate agreed. "Not a long record by any standard. And he'd have had to crank it in order to get it to play. He had to have started it playing, got out of there, and then called right away."

26

"That's why he was so mad," Laura mused. "When you didn't get up and say you were on your way immediately, he thought there was a risk that you weren't going to get here in time. He called this in himself to make sure that you would hear the song when you came onto the crime scene."

"Which means the song is part of it, and this isn't just a random murder by someone who likes old music," Nate said. "It's a message."

"What does it mean?" Officer Munson asked, making them both look around at him.

"I guess that's what we've got to figure out," Laura said. "The first crime scene – you said it was the same?"

"It was," Captain Kinnock said from behind them, clearly taking over from Munson. "That one was found by a member of the public, however."

"How did it happen?" Laura asked. "Wasn't it in an abandoned apartment building? That's what our briefing notes said."

"Right," Kinnock nodded. "But it wasn't going to be abandoned for long. It was scheduled for demolition, and the locals knew about it. A concerned neighbor headed inside when he heard the music playing. He said the song played twice, with a short gap between – the second time was when he went to take a look, thinking it was going to be kids messing around."

"And the scene was the same?" Laura asked.

Kinnock gave a grim nod. "Female victim bound hand and foot, stabbed to death, laying in her own blood in front of the gramophone."

"There was no call on this one?" Laura asked.

"None at all."

She was already developing a theory on that. It seemed altogether possible that the killer set the record going, retreated a short distance, and looked back – to see this concerned neighbor already heading inside. He would have known, then, that it was unnecessary to call. Which begged the question of what he would do in the case of a third murder. Would he call? Leave the body in a place that was more likely to be found? Clearly, leaving it to be discovered long after the record had stopped was not an option.

"What does it mean?" Laura muttered to herself, repeating Officer Munson's question. It was like a scene from a movie – the woman lying on the floor, the sad song playing as a stranger stumbled across her body. Was it all about the drama of it? Something that played into the killer's delusion of himself as a grand or important figure, perhaps? Like a director controlling the scene?

There was a lot to think about, and they had nowhere near enough answers yet to start putting the pieces of the puzzle together.

"Right," Laura said, glancing at Nate. He knew what the next steps were. They always did. They'd been doing this for long enough to know what they had to do now.

"We'd like to talk to the families of the two victims," Nate said. He looked at Captain Kinnock. "Can you give us their addresses? We'll be fine to get ourselves there."

Kinnock nodded. "I'll call in and get them for you," he said.

Laura stepped back from the store and looked up at the sky. The sun was risen now, and there were quiet bird calls somewhere nearby. It looked like the beginning of a nice, mild winter's day. It was totally at odds with the eerie scene that had been set up inside the store.

Laura shivered lightly. There was something about this one…

Whatever it was, she had the feeling that it was going to get more complex, and maybe creepier too, before it was done.

"Let's go, then," Nate said, stepping past her and waving his cell phone – presumably with the addresses of their next two visits saved in it – on the way to the car.

CHAPTER SIX

Laura cleared her throat as they stood waiting for their knock to be answered. It always felt like there wasn't quite enough time to brace yourself fully before you were face-to-face with the grieving family members of your victim. There was nothing like grief, nothing like how it transformed people. And you never knew what stage they would be in – whether they were still in shock or had moved on to something deeper.

The door opened, and Laura braced herself as much as she could, aiming for that smile that was halfway between polite and sympathetic. "Hello," she said. "Mrs. Henson?"

"Yes," she replied, casting a doubtful eye over both Laura and Nate. "I don't want to talk to any journalists."

"Good," Laura said, lifting her badge. "That's a good policy. I'm Special Agent Laura Frost."

"Special Agent Nathaniel Lavoie," Nate added beside her. "We're investigating your daughter's death. Can we come in and ask you a few questions?"

Mrs. Henson's face tightened and drooped. She was very similar to her daughter, from what Laura had seen. She was just older and larger, even though Dakota Henson had been in her twenties – her mother was taller, wider, bigger all around. They did share the same red curls, though, and the same blue eyes – eyes that had been open in fear and pain in the crime scene photographs Laura had seen.

"Come in," Mrs. Henson said at last, stepping aside. She waited for both Laura and Nate to pass her in the narrow corridor so that she could close the door behind them, allowing them to step through into a cramped living room. It was covered on every possible surface by small knick-knacks, figurines and clocks and souvenirs from various parts of the world. It made Laura feel claustrophobic.

There was another person there sitting in an armchair, a young man perhaps around the age that Dakota had been, perhaps a couple of years younger. Laura pegged him as a brother immediately, an idea borne out by an old photograph of two red-headed children above the mantlepiece. He had the same looks as his mother and sister. Laura

29

nodded to him, glancing around, and taking a place right at the far edge of a battered floral sofa. At the other end, a cup of coffee sat on a low table, making her think that this was where Mrs. Henson had been sitting before.

Sure enough, the grieving mother walked past and sat down in that spot, leaving Nate standing. Laura wanted to give him a cunning look indicating that she had been quicker and therefore got the last remaining seat, but it wouldn't have been appropriate if either of the family members in the room had caught her.

"Let me start by saying that we're truly sorry for your loss," Laura said. "To lose a loved one in any circumstance is devastating, but this must be even harder for you. I'm sorry that we're going to have to ask some difficult questions, but we will need to."

Mrs. Henson took a sobbing breath. "We've already spoken to the officers," she said. "Why do we have to go over it again?"

"We're coming to the case with fresh eyes," Laura explained. "It's important that we make sure we haven't missed anything. Please, if you could just bear with us."

"It's for Dakota, Mom," the brother said, and Laura nodded at him gratefully.

Mrs. Henson's shoulders heaved up and down as if to say she had no choice but to agree, her eyes traveling up to that photograph like it was the only thing she could hold onto. Laura shuddered at the thought of having nothing left of her daughter but that, trying to suppress the movement and make it less noticeable.

"Your daughter," Nate said, shifting in his position, awkwardly standing beside the coffee table. "Can you tell us if she had any disagreements with anyone lately? Anyone who had a grudge against her?"

"Of course, not," Mrs. Henson said, shaking her head miserably. "She was a lovely girl. The sweetest. People were always taking advantage of her, but she never even fought back. She was too nice. Everyone liked her."

"I know they all say that," the boy spoke up. "It's the kind of thing you hear on the news all the time, but it's true. Everyone loved 'Kota. She's really – she *was* really nice. I used to rib her about it, tell her she needed to get a backbone."

"Oh, I wish you'd been nicer to her," Mrs. Henson cried, clutching her hands tightly against the hem of her cardigan as if she wanted to wring it out. Her eyes were squeezing shut. She was a woman on the verge of not being able to take much more, Laura could see.

"Sorry, Mom," the boy said quietly, his voice going hoarse.

Blaming one another wasn't a good route to go down – Laura had seen that before. "Did she report anything unusual in the last few weeks?" she asked, trying to change the subject somewhat. "Something that unsettled her or was just different than normal? Someone new hanging around?"

"She didn't say anything." The brother shrugged. "We spoke a couple of days ago. She didn't seem any different. I didn't get the feeling she was hiding anything or whatever."

Laura nodded, looking towards the mother.

"Nothing," Mrs. Henson said. "She said nothing. She was just at home, like normal. That day when she left I didn't even know she'd gone. She sent me a message that she was going to the store and did I want anything, and she never came back."

That wasn't much to go on. Laura tried one last true and tested tactic. "Was she seeing anyone recently?"

"No, not since college," the brother spoke up confidently. "She was kind of aimless the last year or so. With the job market around here the way it is, she was just kind of drifting, looking for something to do."

Laura nodded understanding. That was two questions answered in one: no need to ask about her employment.

"Did she know someone called…" Laura checked the notes from the briefing which she had copied down into her own notebook. "Jenna Janes? Had you heard of her?"

Both the mother and brother shook their heads, exchanging puzzled looks. So, there was no evidence yet that the second victim had known the first one. Of course. It was never going to be that easy, was it?

They were getting a whole lot of nothing right now, which didn't bode well for the overall case.

"Where was she headed?" Laura asked. "Which store?"

"Just at the end of the street, before you get to the school," Mrs. Henson said, nodding in the general direction as though they could see it through the walls of the house.

"Alright," Laura said, getting up. "I think we need to walk the route, take a look at where she was last seen. Thank you for your time – and if you do think of anything that might be helpful, however small, please do get back in touch with us."

31

Mrs. Henson nodded again, her eyes going distant. Laura saw it all the time. The thoughts just seemed to drift out of the minds of those who had suffered a recent loss. Everything, every road, and every thought, led back to the one who was gone. Laura didn't press her on the niceties. She simply nodded once to Mrs. Henson and once to the brother, and then got up to leave.

Nate stepped out by her side as they left the home, so they could walk in tandem. Laura lifted her eyes and nodded forward. The street had a slight rise to it, meaning they could not see where it would take them, but she could see it was long. She estimated it had to be a five-minute walk to the furthest part of the street they could see from where they stood, but from there it was anyone's guess.

"It's eerie," Nate said quietly.

Laura nodded in response. It was a strange feeling, walking in the footsteps of someone who was dead. Even though the circumstances now were far different – they weren't doing anything like a reconstruction of the real events – it sent a shiver down her spine.

"Let's keep our eyes peeled," she said, just to try to break the mood. She began looking while she walked: scanning constantly to the side, looking for anything that might have fallen onto the ground or been trodden into the grass next to the sidewalk, any small sign of what had happened to Dakota Henson. Beside her, Nate did the same, peering down at the side of the road and the drains, covering the area that she couldn't as easily see.

The local cops had already done this, examining the surrounding area as part of their initial investigation, but it didn't hurt to check. It made for slow progress, but as they walked, Laura could finally see the store that Dakota Henson must have been heading for up in front of them. It was a small and unassuming place, and it gave her another shiver to think that this was where the girl must have been taken from. Somewhere along this route – even though the whole time, she would have been in view of other buildings and homes.

"He's bold," Laura said.

"Or maybe cunning," Nate said. He indicated the way the road had that slight angle to it, right behind them. "Look at this view, here. There's not great visibility in either direction. Yes, it's a risk to grab someone here in broad daylight, but it's also not as much of a risk as it might be on any other street. If he had a plan and knew he could grab her quickly, it wouldn't take much."

32

"Or he's neither bold nor cunning but just saw an opportunity and went for it," Laura added. She hoped fervently that her last guess was the most wrong. Opportunistic killers were far harder to catch. Tracking down their motive was near impossible. It was the Ted Bundys of the world that made their job incredibly difficult. Those who killed their friends or relatives or people who had slighted them were so much easier to stop.

They made no further comment as they worked their painstaking way along the route, right up to the front door leading into the store.

"Nothing on my side," Laura said, feeling a little defeated.

"Mine either," Nate responded. "I guess it was too much to hope for at this stage of the investigation."

"Right," Laura agreed. "Do you think she went into the store?"

"I guess the locals would already have figured that out," Nate suggested.

"I'll call," Laura said, grabbing her cell phone out of her pocket. She dialed the number she'd taken down for the captain and waited, glancing around as she did so.

"Captain Kinnock," he said as soon as the line connected.

"Hi," Laura said. "It's Special Agent Frost. Have you ascertained whether Dakota Henson arrived at the store she was heading for or not?"

"Surveillance footage doesn't show her entering," Captain Kinnock replied promptly. "We only have coverage of the entrance – the rest of the street is residential, so no other cameras."

"Right." Laura thought for a minute, about how useless this whole trip had been so far. They'd come to interview the family and learned absolutely nothing new, and the walk to the store had been fruitless as well. They needed to start speeding up, to find the answers they needed quicker. This was taking too long. "Can you tell me if there was anything relevant discovered in the interview with the first victim's family? Jenna Janes?"

"Nothing," Captain Kinnock sighed. "Very similar story to what we learned with the Hensons. Jenna's husband had no answers as to why someone might have targeted her."

Laura chewed her lip, thinking. She looked up at Nate, who held her gaze as if thinking with her. "The setup was exactly the same for Jenna?" she asked.

"Just in a different location," Captain Kinnock replied. "Bound hand and foot, with room to move their hands a little, gramophone and record playing, all the same. Jenna was also abducted and then taken to the location later on."

Laura rubbed her forehead. There wasn't enough data, even though they had two victims already. They just didn't have the information that would separate the two victims, show them why they in particular were chosen, what the killer was trying to say. There must be a link between the two victims in some way, even if it was just that they had been available to the killer *in the same way* when opportunity did strike, but they weren't seeing it yet. And, most frustrating of all, the lack of evidence they could trace to a known person meant they were going to be chasing after him until he made a mistake.

"Thanks," Laura said. "We're going to head to the coroner and take a look at the bodies."

She ended the call, looking up at Nate's semi-amused expression. "We are?" he asked.

"Sorry," she said. She'd made the decision on her own. Maybe she'd grown a little too used to working with rookies and taking charge while he'd been on leave. But it was the only thing that made sense now. "I'm just frustrated with the lack of progress. I figured we look at the bodies next and see what the coroner can tell us. If we don't get anywhere soon, we can circle back around and see what the family of Jenna Janes can tell us later, or look at her crime scene. I don't want to waste too much time on things the locals have already done, though, since they did a thorough enough job here."

Nate nodded his agreement. "Luckily, you're right," he grinned, though the smile lasted only for a moment. Laura could see he felt the same way as she did: that this case wasn't going to solve itself, and if they didn't start to move faster, they weren't either. "Let's go see the coroner."

Laura turned back towards where they had left the car, feeling an itching under her skin that they weren't going fast enough – and determined to do what she could to catch up.

CHAPTER SEVEN

The coroner's office turned out to be underground, beneath the precinct, taking advantage of the cooler tunnels under the earth to aid in storing the bodies of those who needed examination.

The coroner, however, was nowhere to be seen.

"Hello?" Laura called out again for what felt like the seventeenth time. She bent forward over the front desk, trying to see if there was a button she could press or some way she could let them in through the locked door.

"It's pointless," Nate said. "Maybe we should go check something else out first and then come back with Captain Kinnock."

"Check out what?" Laura asked, exasperated beyond measure. "And even if we go get the captain, who knows if he can actually get in himself?"

"He can't, actually."

Laura spun around to see a tall, thin man in a white lab coat approaching them. He was licking his fingers on his right hand, and had what appeared to be a small metal lunchbox in an old-fashioned style in his left.

"You're the coroner?" Nate asked, sizing the guy up immediately.

"I am," he confirmed, in a casual manner. He stood sharply, almost clicking his heels as he snapped into a military posture, drawing himself up. "Ian. I'm guessing you're the FBI agents I've been waiting for."

"That would be us," Laura confirmed. She eyed his lunchbox, wondering what on earth he was up to.

"I've been having lunch," Ian clarified. His dark hair was slicked back over his head and away from his glasses, giving him what had to be a textbook nerd look. But, like Captain Kinnock, Laura had to guess he was unusually young for his position.

"It's eleven in the morning," Nate pointed out.

"Yes, well, I start early," Ian said, sweeping past them towards the door that had been locked until now. He produced a swipe card from his pocket and opened it with a flourish. "And thankfully, my workmates don't tend to mind when or how long I go out on a break for."

A blast of cooler air hit Laura as she followed Ian into the morgue, Nate coming up behind her. There was also a very particular smell: mostly cleaning fluid, along with something strong and minty that Laura identified as probably some kind of air freshener. She had found in her many travels, occasionally, coroners who liked their morgue to have a particular scent to mask that of the bodies.

"Right," Ian said, dropping his lunchbox onto a desk in the corner with a clang that made Laura jump. "Who would you like to see first? Miss Janes, or Miss Henson?"

They'd already seen so much of Dakota Henson's life, it would be interesting to get a view of the other victim. "Janes," Laura said – at exactly the same time as Nate. They looked at one another with a spark of amusement in their eyes. Even when one of them was attempting to take charge, it seemed, they both had the same ideas anyway.

"Janes it is," Ian said, whirling around and trotting right to the exact drawer they wanted and pulling it out.

She was a shocking sight, as all bodies invariably were. Laura had seen so many of them in her career, but that didn't take the sting away completely, even if it did deaden her senses a little. When the victims were young or beautiful, or both, it was more difficult. There was something about a life snatched down in its prime that was just harder to take.

And Jenna Janes, for her part, had certainly been beautiful. She was older than Dakota Henson and yet still younger than Laura herself. She must have married early in life. Vibrant red hair framed her face even in death – Ian had fanned it out over the metal drawer as if she was posing for a photoshoot set in a morgue, not laying in one.

"She looks asleep," Nate commented. It was a fair point to bring up: often when they dealt with murder victims, the body wasn't so pretty in more ways than one. There would be a slit throat, a bashed-in skull, a gunshot wound to the head. But Jenna really did look perfectly asleep and still, without a mark on her face or shoulders.

Until Ian flipped back the sheet to the bottom of her torso, revealing the large stab wound right through the point above her heart.

"Not anymore, she doesn't," Laura murmured. It was a horrible thing – a mark that spoiled everything. Even though the blood had been washed away, leaving the wound strangely white, it stood out on

Jenna's chest as a blight, matching the marks left by the coroner's examination.

"As you can see, death was conclusively caused by a stab wound to the heart," the coroner said. "She wouldn't have lasted long after being stabbed. The killer knows what he's doing. He's used a strong degree of accuracy both here and in the case of the other victim. Right down with a blade wide enough to pierce essentially the whole of the heart, bringing about cessation of function with immediacy when the blade is withdrawn."

"She wouldn't have suffered, then," Laura said. There was something about Jenna's haunting beauty that made her glad about it. That she wouldn't have wanted this woman to suffer.

"She might have, I'm afraid," the coroner said, pointing downwards to draw their attention further. "She has rope burns to the wrists and ankles where she was restrained. This suggests there was a certain amount of movement before she was killed – that she perhaps tried to escape or run. It's the same in the other case. If I was to describe the scene of their deaths, I would say they were looking up from a prone position on the floor, perhaps trying to crawl backwards away from him, and they saw him bring the sword down on them. Oh, and there's also some bruising to the hips and back in both cases, suggesting they were pushed down to the floor from a higher position with enough force to cause an impact."

Laura shook her head silently, seeing Nate do the same in her peripheral vision. Whoever this was, this killer, he had some kind of agenda. He had to. There was pattern to this. It wasn't just a mad frenzy – not like the Ted Bundys of the world she had thought of earlier. With careful and considered method, there was often reason, logic. A twisted logic that only a madman would understand, but…

Ian turned away to gesture to another drawer, and Laura brushed her hand against Jenna Janes's hand surreptitiously. She waited for the headache that always signaled one of her visions was about to start, but nothing came. It rarely did, with the bodies, no matter how much she wanted it to. There was nothing in Jenna Janes's future. Nothing for her visions to predict.

"Do you want to see the other one? It's the same story," Ian said.

"No, thank you," Nate replied, choosing for both of them. "I think we've seen enough."

Laura nodded. She had. The coroner's expert opinion was what they really needed here, and they had it. If touching the body gave her

37

nothing, Laura was going to have to wait and find something else. Ideally, something the killer had touched.

A murder weapon would have been wonderful, but of course they wouldn't be that lucky yet.

"Let's go find Captain Kinnock," Nate suggested. "Get ourselves set up at a desk and look everything over."

"Sure," Laura agreed. But she had the uneasy feeling that what they had so far was a whole bunch of nothing.

***

Laura adjusted the chair she'd been lent by one of the detectives in the precinct, uncomfortable in more ways than one. She hated it when they were given a desk in the middle of the bullpen instead of a private office. She could always just feel everyone staring at her. Looking at the FBI agents. Resenting, or wondering, or idolizing – whatever the reason, she didn't enjoy the scrutiny one bit.

Still, they had to go with the space that the precinct had available – and apparently, this was it.

"Let's go over everything piece by piece," Nate suggested. "So, from what we know, he abducts them when they're alone and vulnerable."

"So far, we've probably narrowed it down to every single serial killer ever who's used abduction," Laura said drily. "If it was me, I don't think I'd choose to abduct someone who was in a large group of friends and heavily armed."

"I'm just laying out the facts," Nate said, giving her a sour look. Laura tried to rein her own disappointment in and stop taking it out on him. "He takes them to an abandoned location. That part, he has to scout ahead of time, right?"

"Right," Laura nodded. "That's the only thing we can say for sure is premeditated – location and method. Once he has them, he knows what he's doing. I'm just not sure whether he chooses them carefully or goes for whatever he can take."

Nate nodded agreement. "He must have the gramophone, record, and the weapon ready when he arrives. I'm guessing the rope, too. I'm trying to figure out the logistics. Maybe he grabs them, throws them in a car or van, and then ties them up when he gets them out? It would be a risk, though, of someone fighting him off and escaping."

"Not if he knocks them out," Laura said. "We didn't ask the coroner about bloodstream analysis – whether they were drugged or something."

Nate nodded. "Town like this, it'll probably be a little while before they get the results back," he said. "I didn't see any lab equipment in the morgue."

"Me either," Laura sighed. At least if there were any further tests required, they could expedite things by sending them off to an FBI lab. "But we can assume he has some method of keeping them calm, somehow. Either drugs, or maybe some kind of promise or... I don't know. A confidence trick? A lot of killers in the past have dressed up as law enforcement."

"This is too much speculation," Nate said, shaking his head. "We're going to end up chasing our own tails instead of getting anywhere close to the killer. The first thing we need to do is get the lab results back and see if they were drugged, and if they weren't, then we start thinking about alternate possibilities."

"Agreed," Laura said. "I guess we need to look at the MO instead. What he's doing and how, once he actually has them. But I don't get it. This gramophone, the song – I don't know what he's trying to tell us."

"Maybe he's not trying to tell us anything," Nate said, with a wry smile in her direction. "Maybe he knows what he means and that's enough."

"That doesn't help us much," Laura said, sighing. "Where do we go next?"

"Well..." Nate cast a glance all around and then lowered his voice. "It would be mighty useful to know what the killer was up to right now."

Laura knew what he meant. *It would be useful if you had a vision.* Which was all well and good – but she was going to have to think of something that would trigger one.

Easier said than done, Laura thought, burying her head in her hands for a minute to think.

The evidence locker, she thought, snapping her head up – that was where she needed to go next. That was the only place she was going to get any answers.

CHAPTER EIGHT

He sat down on the bare wooden boards of the attic and rested, feeling the peace of the silent space fill him for a moment as it always did. He needed it, today. He needed to breathe in the dust of the old memories there, to smell the past.

He rested his wrists across his knees, legs curled up in front of himself, feet crossed over on the floor. He could have leaned to one side or the other and put his weight onto one of the boxes around him, but he did not want to disturb their slumber. The gramophones were silent, waiting for their time. He saw them like elderly old performers, saving their energy for that one last show. He would let them rest until then.

He let his eyes drift closed, breathing in the familiar air of the space. The attic was a special spot for him. A place he could connect with the past, make it part of the present. It was almost meditative. Another deep breath, and he let his eyes slide open lazily to take in the form of the edges of one of the gramophones.

He remembered dancing around the tiled floor downstairs, his bare feet and his grandmother's, whirling around in time to the music. The way they swayed together to the old familiar tunes, always in silence. Sometimes she would sing along, her voice trembling and weak but the finest thing he had ever heard. She would hook up one of her beauties every week – that was what she called them – and then they would dance, and for a while everything would be fine.

He imagined them there in the space above him, the dancing dust motes in the air a background for their silent show. How he swayed first reaching up for her hands, then later reaching down, holding her. He remembered how she would smile and sigh when she heard the music.

Until they listened to that song.

Every time, it was the end of the smiles and laughter. Every time, she would go still and quiet, then turn on him and yell. He was never good enough. He hadn't cleaned his room. He hadn't finished the food she lovingly prepared for him. He hadn't had the top grades in his class at school.

He tried so hard to be a good boy, but no matter what he did, he never seemed able to overcome his one major flaw in her eyes.

That he had been born male.

He closed his eyes to shut the memory out again, watching himself fall to the floor in the wake of her slap and not wanting to see what came next. When he opened them again he was alone in the attic, the gramophones waiting around him like silent companions.

He blinked a few times like he was waking up and nodded to himself. He reached into the pocket of his jacket and drew out a few folded pieces of paper, opening them and smoothing them out onto the wooden boards in front of him. They matched up exactly with the disturbed edges of the dust, the outlines of where he had placed them last time he was up here.

He studied the map carefully, poring over it. He had marked out a number of locations that he knew would work, places where he could take them. He had to take them somewhere, and these places were exactly what he needed. Quiet, out of the way, somewhere they wouldn't be disturbed. But when the dancing was over, he needed to be sure they would be found.

He glanced over the spots again and tapped one of them, one he had marked out recently. He knew it was the right one to head for next. It was obvious to him that it fit perfectly, and there was no sense in waiting. The way things were going now, all in order like it was always meant to be that way, he wasn't going to argue.

He studied the other pieces of paper briefly and then gave a decisive nod, folding them back up and replacing them in his pocket. He looked up then at the nearest gramophone, and gave it a reassuring pat. Soon, its time would come. It was nearly time for it to play for the last time.

CHAPTER NINE

Laura closed her eyes and tried to think. What was the most likely to give her a result?

She had managed to get a good look at the evidence locker, and she'd managed to persuade the cop on duty to leave her alone there. It wasn't strictly protocol, but she figured that he saw an FBI badge and thought she outranked him anyway. She wasn't going to dissuade him otherwise.

Which meant that now she had access to every item belonging to the victims that had been recovered from the scene – everything that hadn't been taken into the lab for testing – and everything recovered from their homes that was deemed to be useful. The problem was, she couldn't touch all of them.

No matter what she touched, it was a risk. The evidence would be contaminated with her fingerprints, meaning that any testing carried out on it later would show that she had touched it. That would get any evidentiary value it had reduced to nothing, as any good defense lawyer would throw it out of the courtroom immediately. Not only that, but it could open the jury up to suggestions of evidence tampering and thus cast a shadow of doubt over any other evidence that she'd had access to. It could risk the whole case if they couldn't get a suspect to plead guilty.

Nevertheless, it was a risk she wanted to take. Because if she didn't, she wasn't going to get anywhere. She needed to do something to trigger a vision. She and Nate were stuck, completely lost, and there was no visible way forward that didn't include simply going over and over things the locals had already examined in detail. If she had a vision of where the killer was going to go next, or who he would target, or even where he got the gramophones from – anything would help.

But the question was, which of the evidence items spread out on the desk in front of her was worth the risk to get it out of the plastic bag and contaminate it? Which would have the least impact on the case and yet the most likelihood of yielding a vision?

In some ways, it was lucky that the two victims so far had both been women. They carried purses, which had been found left at the scene. There were so many different items in there that were personal – lipsticks, home and car keys, wallets, even phones. But then again, none of these necessarily had any connection to the killer, and that was what Laura needed. The last thing she wanted was to end up getting a vision of the past again and seeing something from when the victim was a child, which would be no help to anyone.

There was one option, though. A coat which one of the victims had been wearing. It had been left to the side of one of the rooms, discarded because it didn't fit into the killer's vision. Laura was sure it had already been checked for fingerprints and fibers and found to be of no value, or it wouldn't be here – it would be at the lab with the other things. But if the killer had touched it, even with gloves on…

It would be a link to him that might trigger a vision.

She cast a glance over her shoulder and checked that no one was anywhere near entering the room, then moved quick as a flash. She unzipped the plastic evidence bag and grabbed the coat, plunging her hand inside the bag instead of taking the coat all the way out.

Nothing.

She took a breath. She'd touched it now. There was no going back. Might as well go forward. She let go and tried another spot, then another – the lapel, the zipper, the pocket, the toggle – a headache struck her temple, shooting around inside her skull, and she only had time to –

She was standing a short distance away from Zach, who was laying on the ground. Zach, who was looking up in terror. Zach, with Chris crouching over him, kneeling on him, over his chest, pinning him down.

No, Laura thought, but she was powerless. She couldn't move, breathe, speak, do anything to stop it from happening. She could only watch, unable to tear her eyes away, as Chris raised his right arm in the air. The edges of the vision were fuzzy and black, like so many of them had been lately. And then Chris plunged his arm down, his hand going right into Zach's chest, stabbing him…

Laura blinked and gasped for air, snatching her hand out of the evidence bag and zipping it back up before anyone could come in and see her. She replaced the items back into the large box they had been stored in, one after the other, almost throwing them in her haste. She wanted to be free and clear of them before she stopped.

Then she did stop, trying to catch her breath, leaning on the edge of the table for support.

Why was she still seeing the same thing?

This wasn't supposed to be how it worked. She was supposed to see something related to the case – to the killer. Not something random from her own life. She'd *never* triggered an unrelated vision before. It just didn't happen.

But then neither did many of the other things she'd been experiencing lately. Foggy visions with black around the edges until she could barely make out what was going on. Visions of the past. Visions that misled her by appearing to be something else. It was all wrong, all of it – and one of the worst things was that the visions didn't seem to want to come at all.

Laura took a long, heavy breath, stabilizing herself, trying to get her heartbeat and her breathing under control. She was going to have to figure this thing out soon – very soon, because if the visions she was seeing were going to come true, she wouldn't have Zach around for much longer at all.

***

Nate shifted restlessly in front of the computer screen, drumming his fingers on the desk. Part of him wanted to get up and follow Laura and see what she was doing, but he hadn't been invited. He didn't take offense at that. It was just something she had to do alone, whatever it was.

He thought he knew, anyway. She was probably trying to do something to trigger a vision. And if she hadn't invited him along for that, it was probably because having him around was putting her off. He'd noticed that she hadn't had many visions at all since he found out about them, and that had to be no coincidence.

But it did leave him twiddling his thumbs, as it were, and he needed to think of something to do that would be useful.

Research. He could always try and do a bit of research.

Nate hit the mouse to wake up the screen, then cracked his knuckles. He could do this. There had to be an angle here, a way to attack the problem and figure out a solution. He just had to find the way in. And the most obvious thing, to him, had to be the gramophones.

Gramophones weren't exactly a usual household item these days. They'd gone out of style decades ago. You didn't see them just anywhere – they were more likely to be museum exhibits than anything else. But this guy had not one gramophone, but two. Identical ones, and historically dated. Not replicas. The original, real thing.

That had to be hard to get hold of. Surely, it would be possible to track down someone who had purchased two – and maybe more.

At least, much more possible than finding a match for their prints when all they knew about the suspect so far was that he wasn't in the database.

"Alright," Nate muttered to himself, typing the simplest starting point he could think of into his search engine: *buy antique gramophone*.

A few results came up. He wasn't surprised, really, by what he saw. The first few were various auction and online sales sites, the kind that seemed to sell everything to everyone these days. So far, so predictable. But those sites, while a good resource for someone who was a casual collector, wouldn't be enough for the more serious type. They probably weren't a good start for someone who wanted multiple identical devices, either. For that, you'd want to go to a dealer.

There were a good few antiques dealers coming up in the first few pages of results, but Nate knew he didn't have time to go through all of them one by one. He needed to narrow the field down.

If you were buying something as heavy and delicate as a gramophone, you wouldn't ship it from the other side of the world, would you? Not unless you had some serious cash to throw around. And, while there was the odd exception, it had always seemed to Nate that the kind of men who became serial killers weren't the rich and successful type.

He typed in *antique gramophone Maryland* and tried again.

This time, there were only a few results that popped up that had actual map locations. He clicked on the first one and browsed around on their site, only to see that they didn't actually sell gramophones specifically – it was probably just a search term they'd included on their website to try and hook any and all collectors of antique goods. The second one turned out to have closed down three years ago, which made them an unlikely candidate for the purchases.

But the third one gave him pause.

It was an antiques dealer who specialized in audio equipment – old sound machines like phonographs, early recorders, vintage records, and gramophones. That was incredibly promising. The site promised to buy any and all antique devices and also to offer a wide array of the same, fully restored with original parts, to collectors.

Huh.

Nate glanced around, looking for a printer in the bullpen, but in the end he gave up and grabbed his notebook to write down the address. There was no point in trying to print something and then spending the next half hour figuring out which printer it had gone to. Offices like this were all the same – law enforcement or not, there was always some complex and outdated IT structure that would leave you scratching your head and having to snag some passing assistant for help, only to get your head snapped off for interrupting their own workload.

Not that this had happened before, or anything.

Nate glanced up after finishing his notes to see Laura making her way across the bullpen from the other side of the room, her shoulders slumped in what looked like defeat. She reached the desk without a word and slumped down into a chair beside him, clearly in no mood to mess around.

"No luck?" Nate asked, guessing now for sure that she'd been in search of a vision.

"Nothing," Laura confirmed. "I just can't… *see* anything that will take us forward in the case."

Nate nodded at her carefully coded language, letting her know he understood. "Well, this might cheer you up. I have a local antiques dealer who specializes in things like gramophones. I was thinking we ought to go down there and ask to see their records."

"Where is it?" Laura asked, sitting up in the chair.

"Well, that's the best part," Nate said with a grin. "You know, I don't believe in coincidences. And this antiques dealer happens to be based right here in town."

He clearly didn't need to tell Laura twice. She jumped up from her chair and then looked back at him, cocking her head. "Well? Aren't you going to come and check it out?"

Nate grinned and got up to follow her, swiping his notebook and the address from the desk as he went.

CHAPTER TEN

Laura looked up at the store from the car, wondering what they were about to walk into.

"That's kind of unusual," she said, stating the obvious.

"Yeah," was all Nate could manage in return.

The storefront was almost obnoxious in declaring what it was. It was only a small store, from the outside at least, but the frames around the door and windows and a large wooden signage area above the door were painted an electric shade of blue. On top of this signage was painted not only the words *Antique Sound*, but also several large musical instruments from times gone by. And not just painted, either – the blue illustrations were three-dimensional, actual wooden models attached to the storefront in an exaggerated size. Above it all was a huge black half-record with a bright pink center, as if to attract as much attention as possible from anywhere you stood in the town.

"Let's see if we can find the owner," Laura suggested, unbuckling her seatbelt, and reaching for the door handle.

"If he's painted the same colors, we'll spot him a mile off," Nate muttered before following her.

Laura pushed the door of the store open to the tinkling chime of a bell, and glanced around. It looked pretty much like how she expected an antiques store to look. Everything was dusty and old-looking, shelves and floors stacked with example after example of old musical instruments, music players, sheet music, and stacks of records in colorful sleeves. There was a counter, too – but for the moment, it was empty.

Laura glanced around, wondering if there was a bell or something she could press, as Nate entered behind her. The door swung shut and made the bell tinkle again, announcing their presence for a second time. Laura hoped that, at least, would be enough to make someone appear.

A moment later, they did: a tall, thin man who could almost have been the cousin of their coroner, Ian, although significantly older. And odder, too, at first glance. Laura took him in with a look as she strode towards him, reaching into her pocket to pull out her badge. He was dressed in a formal and stiff black suit with a starched white shirt, the

47

only flash of color about him at all being a pocket handkerchief in the same color as the storefront. He had dark hair slicked back with what looked like old-fashioned pomade, and his cheeks were gauntly hollow.

"Can I help you?" he asked.

"Yes," Laura said, taking her first real breath of the air within the closed environment of the store. It almost choked her. It was musty and the air seemed laden with dust that stirred at their every move. It was an asthma sufferer's nightmare. She put her badge down on the counter in front of him, noticing the warped and marked wood of it as she did so. "I'm Special Agent Laura Frost. We're in town investigating a serious crime."

"I would assume so," he said, though there was a note of interest in his voice. "I gather the FBI doesn't come out to investigate small crimes."

"That's correct," Nate said, stepping forward. He flashed his badge, but didn't put it down like Laura had. "Special Agent Nathaniel Lavoie. I read online that you sell gramophones here."

"We do," he said, perking up. His back seemed to go even straighter, if that were possible. "We have all kinds of models here. Many of them are in good working order."

"All originals?" Nate asked.

"Of course," he said, seeming to take offense. "I wouldn't sell cheap modern imitations."

"Right, of course," Laura said, trying to mollify him before he took them off on some tangent about the state of the gramophone industry. "We're looking to see if there are any customers who have bought from you recently. They would have made at least two purchases of the same gramophone. Do you recall anyone like that?"

He frowned slightly. "Am I allowed to tell you that?"

"We're FBI agents," Laura said, finding herself frowning at him. "What was your name, sir?"

"Artur Oreyo," he said, drawing himself up once again. Then, he delivered a stiff and formal nod. "At your service. I just wasn't sure if I would be breaking some kind of customer confidentiality accord."

"Like I said, we're investigating a very serious crime," Laura told him. She was starting to feel impatient. Usually when it took this long to get someone to agree to fetch their records, it was because they were trying to hide something. What was going on here? "If you could show us your customer purchase records, that would be fantastic."

Artur cleared his throat, and from the sound and movement behind the desk, Laura could almost swear he had clicked his heels together smartly. "We keep paper records," he said. "I know it's a bit old-fashioned, but I don't like to have modern machinery anywhere near my vintage beauties. It upsets the balance of things. It might be a little difficult for you to go through everything."

Why did Laura get the feeling that he was trying to avoid bringing them out? "All the same, we'd like to see them."

Artur nodded with an uncomfortable expression, like he was straining too hard to keep the polite smile on his face. "I'll fetch them from the back room. How many years of sales would you like?"

"Just one would be fine," Nate said, and Laura could sense a tension in the thick muscles of his neck that suggested he was probably trying to resist turning to look at her incredulously.

Then Artur glided away through a black curtain behind the counter and out of sight again, and Nate turned to give her that exact look she had been expecting.

Laura shot him a warning glance of her own and moved closer, stepping around a box of old cassette tapes until she was right next to him. "He might still be able to hear us," she whispered.

"I don't like him," Nate whispered back. "He's got a vibe."

"A vibe?" Laura said with a sideways smirk, though she knew exactly what he was talking about. There was something off about Artur Oreyo, like he was from a distant era. Someone obsessed with the past. Maybe it just went with the territory of being an antique store owner, but...

Maybe it was the hallmark of a killer who seemed to want to create some kind of macabre old Hollywood scene with every life he took.

Laura started to walk between the rows of shelving and stacked equipment in the store. It was dim inside and hard to see until you were right up close to the shelves; it was as though Oreyo didn't want any light to come in and damage his precious antiques. Laura didn't know much about preserving them, but it did seem odd that he wouldn't have the overhead lights switched on brightly to make up for it. How else would his customers see what they were going to buy?

Laura ran her hands idly over a shelf of records, feeling how the thin spines stacked against one another. She started to flip through them, looking at the titles on the fronts of the covers. Most of them, she'd never heard of before. Old songs, judging by the fonts and the way the paper was yellowed and faded. Most of them didn't even have pictures on the front, just words.

They all had those fascinating old titles, too, making Laura wonder about what the songs must sound like. *Way Down in Old Milwaukee Way, Time for a Change of Heart, The New Dance That Everybody Loves.*

And then she stopped, her hand hovering ready to push the next one aside, unable to quite believe what she was seeing.

"Nate," she hissed.

He came to her side quickly, putting down some kind of brass horn with a clatter. He looked at what she had found and gave a low whistle. "*My Man and the Rose* by Nena Flora," he read aloud. "That's the song."

"Isn't it supposed to be kind of rare? All but forgotten, these days?" Laura whispered.

"Yeah," Nate said. "But, just to play devil's advocate, isn't that exactly the type of thing you'd normally find in an antique record store?"

"Yes," Laura said, glancing over her shoulder to check that Oreyo wasn't back yet. "But he's taking an awfully long time, and I didn't get the sense he wanted to show us his books. And he has that vibe."

"Yeah," Nate said. He paused, his hand traveling to his hip to check that his gun was still holstered there under his jacket. "Maybe I should go back and see what's taking so long."

There was a short pause as Nate began to walk towards the counter, and then Oreyo exploded from out of the black curtain with a theatrical wave of his hand. "I have it!" he exclaimed, and Laura found her own hand going to her hip too, her racing heart only cooling down when she realized he was being melodramatic and not threatening.

"We'd like to ask you a few questions as well," Nate said, reaching out for the black leather-bound record book in Oreyo's hands and taking it. "Where were you yesterday around two in the afternoon?"

That was the time they knew Dakota Henson had left home and walked down the street towards the store, only to be abducted by her killer.

"I was here," Oreyo answered immediately. "I always am, on weekdays. From nine in the morning through to six at night. When I don't have customers, I work on cleaning and restoring my new finds."

"Did you have any customers yesterday?" Nate asked, and Laura knew he meant 'witnesses.'

50

"No," Oreyo admitted slowly. "We've started to do a bit of online business, you see, so people don't have to come down here anymore."

Laura almost rolled her eyes. He was trying to defend his business, but she couldn't care less whether he was making enough money or not. "Is there a camera anywhere in here?"

"No," he said again. "I told you. I don't like to have modern equipment near my antiques."

"Mr. Oreyo, you're making it a little difficult for us to confirm your alibi," Nate said, folding his arms over his chest.

"Oh, I was here!" Oreyo replied, his eyes wide. "There's a camera across the street that covers the door. You could check that. You'll see the store was open all day long and I never left."

A camera covering the door wouldn't be much help if he needed to accuse someone of theft. Laura narrowed her eyes, wondering. Was he trying to hide something going on inside his business? Or was it just that a business like this didn't make enough money to install a camera? Or – the reason he'd given – was he really so old-fashioned he didn't want a camera in the store?

"We'll be checking," Nate promised, making a mark in his notebook. Laura made her own mental note to ask one of the local cops back at the precinct to check it out so they could focus on other leads. Watching footage was the kind of job that could take hours, and you had to keep up your concentration the whole way through – not the best task for the lead agents on the case to take on. "Now, your customer records. Do you recall anyone who bought multiple gramophones in one transaction? Or even anyone who purchased multiples across different purchases?"

"I can answer that question for you right now and take my books back," Oreyo said, eyeing them in Nate's hand. Laura was beyond convinced now that there was something funny going on with the business. Some kind of tax evasion, most likely. "I have the customer information off the top of my head, because it only happened last week. And it's the only instance I can recall in the last ten years of a customer buying more than one. You normally only need one to play your records, so it's rare to sell two, let alone three."

"Three?" Nate asked, his eyebrows shooting up as he glanced at Laura. Three was good news and bad news. Good, because it would make it very simple to track down a good, strong suspect. Bad, because it would mean there was one more gramophone left that hadn't been used.

"Do we have a deal?" Oreyo asked, looking at the book in Nate's hand expectantly.

Nate hesitated for just a moment, clearly weighing up the risk and reward. Laura wished she'd had a vision to help, but nothing in the dusty shelves of the store had stirred a reaction in her mind. "Fine," he said, at last, handing the book back over. "But you better have an address for us."

"Address, name, and telephone number," Oreyo said. He opened the book to one specific page and spun it around to show them the notes scratched on the paper – a scrawled receipt, it looked like, with all the customer's information. "Yvan, that was his name. He paid in cash, so I don't have a credit card record, but I remember his name. It was unusual enough. And I took his address so that I could deliver the items to his home."

"Did you take them personally?" Nate asked.

"No, I ordered a specialist courier," Oreyo said. He tore out the page of the book with quick, precise movements, taking it so neatly it didn't even look as though there had been a page there to start with. Laura looked down, but he closed the book smartly enough before she could see what was on the page behind it. "They package everything very carefully and make sure there's no damage in transit."

Nate glanced over the piece of paper with the address – it was blank on the other side, as if Oreyo only used the right-hand pages of the book – and then folded it into his pocket. "How did you order that?"

"Over the internet," Oreyo said, and then stopped abruptly. He colored, his cheeks shading in red.

"If you're prepared to stretch to Wi-Fi, maybe consider stretching to a security camera," Nate said, shaking his head. "You'll thank me if you ever get a thief in here."

He turned to Laura who nodded. "We'll be in touch if we need anything else," she said, figuring it wouldn't hurt to stick a pin in Oreyo and come back to him later. After all, if the gramophones and the record continued to be important, an antiques dealer who specialized in sound would be a good expert to come to.

For now, though, they had a much more pressing matter. This Yvan, whoever he was, seemed like a very good suspect already, and they didn't even know anything about him. And the quicker they got to him, maybe the quicker they could stop him taking that third life.

CHAPTER ELEVEN

"Right," Laura said, putting the phone down. "The detective found him. His full name is Yvan West. He doesn't have a criminal record, but he's been registered at that address for a couple of decades."

"No record," Nate nodded. "That explains why we couldn't find a match for the prints."

"Maybe," Laura said. She was feeling an abundance of caution, for some reason. Maybe because it was very early in the case, and they'd gone from no leads at all to suddenly having a viable suspect. She was probably just being paranoid, she told herself. Looking for the downside. No, he was going to be their killer.

Maybe she just wanted this to be wrong so that she wouldn't have to go back home and face the whole Zach/Chris dilemma again.

"Well?" Nate asked. "You want to get backup, or go straight in?"

Laura bit her lip, looking down the street at the home they were staking out. Watching the place while they checked out the details of the registered homeowner meant they could be sure he hadn't left to go and kill someone else while they did what essentially amounted to paperwork.

The street was quiet as the day stretched into evening. Most people had come home from work already, a few of them even while Laura and Nate watched from their car. There was already a vehicle outside of the property registered to Yvan West, the place where the gramophones had been delivered, and it hadn't moved.

"I think we should go in alone," she said. "It's a quiet, residential place. He won't know that we're coming. I think if we go in all guns blazing, we'll cause more problems than we solve. Quick, quiet, and efficient is best."

"Hm." Nate chewed his own lip for a moment before looking back at Laura. "Fine. But at the first sign of anything going south, we retreat and call for backup. No heroics, alright?"

Laura glanced at him. "Is this because I got hit in the head last time?"

"And burned the time before that," Nate said, gesturing to the side of her hand. She was still wearing a bandage there, though a very light one. It was getting along towards healed. "Not to mention all the other times. Laura, you kind of have a reckless approach to arresting suspects."

Laura shrugged. "I just don't want anyone else to die," she said, looking away from the bandage. She hardly thought about it anymore. There was always something more pressing – a case, Lacey, a date with Chris, her visions. It was only when she had to go back to the hospital to get the dressing changed and the progress checked that it bothered her.

"Yeah, well, I don't want *you* to die," Nate said, starting the engine. "So sue me. I'm going to pull up right outside so we can get him out here in cuffs easier, alright?"

"Right," Laura agreed, finding no reason to argue with him about the other thing and prolong the discussion.

Nate did as he said he would, slowly creeping the car forward and then pulling to a stop directly outside the home. Laura eyed the door, the front yard, the car parked in the driveway. She was mentally assessing, looking for escape routes they'd have to watch out for, things that might go wrong.

"Ready?"

Laura nodded. "Ready."

The two of them got out of the car in tandem, timing it well to slam their doors shut in the same moment. Laura was on the passenger side and therefore the fastest to walk up the short path to the front door, but Nate was right behind her as she knocked loudly and forcefully. She waited a moment, listening hard. She wasn't against the idea of breaking the door down if no one answered. They had reasonable suspicion that someone could be held captive in there even right now, after all.

But then she heard a footstep on the other side of the door, and felt every muscle in her body tense for the confrontation.

It was a man that answered the door, which was a good start – but she had no idea yet what their suspect looked like. "Yvan West?" she asked, barking the words louder than she'd intended.

"Yes," he said, looking taken aback, glancing between her and Nate on his doorstep.

"FBI," Nate announced, quickly moving forward to put himself in the doorway so that West couldn't close it. "We have some questions to ask you. Alright if we come inside?" He was already moving, forcing

West to walk back with him in the narrow corridor, keeping him away from the door and the exit to potential freedom.

"Um," West managed, beginning to stammer. Laura stepped in after Nate and closed the door behind her. Perhaps they were being heavy-handed, but not if they were dealing with a killer who had already taken multiple lives. "Wh-what's going on – who are you -?"

"Take a seat, Mr. West," Nate said, deftly finding the living room and gesturing their suspect towards a sofa. He sat obediently, almost falling down as if he had no control over whether he obeyed or not. The house was cramped inside, filled with too much furniture, most of which was also covered in boxes and stacked organizers. What was this?

"What's happening?" Mr. West asked again, almost plaintively.

Laura glanced around and her heart almost stopped.

Right in the front of the living room, tucked inside a bay window with the curtains resting right up against them, were three devices that looked like they played music. But they were not gramophones.

"What are those?" Laura asked bluntly, doing nothing to assuage his fears just yet. If he was on the back foot, and not putting on a performance, so much the better. They didn't want him to think he could get the upper hand on them if he really was the killer.

"Phonographs," he said. "They're an old kind of record player. I- I work at the community theater in town and we thought they might add a bit of class to our performances, but we needed three, you see – two to run in alternate scenes and one in case the others break down." He was rambling, seemingly with nerves, his words fast and running into one another.

And Laura had a very bad feeling.

"Where did you get those from?" she asked.

"Antique Sound, over on Rose Avenue," West said.

Laura's stomach dropped even further.

"Have you purchased anything else from that store?" she asked.

"N-no," West stammered, looking utterly bewildered. "Is there some kind of problem with the store? I only discovered it last week. It's my first time buying anything there."

Nate swore under his breath.

"Let me be absolutely clear about this," Laura said, looking him dead in the eye. "You purchased three phonographs from Antique Sound last week. You didn't purchase any gramophones?"

"No!" West said. "No, just the phonographs. I – I have a receipt around here somewhere, I can show you!"

Laura drew a heavy sigh. West was hovering uncertainly, halfway off the sofa with his arms in the air like he thought he was going to get shot if he moved too fast.

"He got the machines mixed up," Laura said. "Phonographs, not gramophones. They look alike, but they're not the ones we're looking for."

Nate threw his head back and groaned in frustration, and then rubbed his face. "Mr. West, please forgive the intrusion," he said. "It seems this has been a case of mistaken identity."

"So, I'm not in trouble?" West asked. "Do you still need the receipt?"

"If you could," Nate said, as Laura stepped off to the side, unable to bear it. They'd hit another dead end. The only lead they had, and it had turned out to be nothing.

What the hell were they going to do now?

CHAPTER TWELVE

Laura rested her hands on the steering wheel, listening to the faint sound of the engine cooling down, and sighed.

"I know," Nate said. "But it's late. And you said it yourself yesterday. We work better when we're rested."

"If we had done any actual work today, I would probably feel better about that idea," Laura scowled.

Nate shook his head. In the darkness of the parking lot, they were the only people around. Laura felt exposed under the car's interior light, like everyone in the motel rooms above would be watching them. "We did a lot of work today," he said. "It just feels like we didn't because we haven't caught the guy yet."

Laura looked at her hands under the artificial yellow light. She'd had no vision today. Well, nothing about the case. It felt like that was all her life was lately. A constant stream of disappointment about not having the right visions. Even when she did, she was misinterpreting them.

Not for the first time and almost certainly not for the last, Laura wanted a drink.

"Tomorrow's a new day," Nate said, still trying to reassure her. "We're going to get something tomorrow. Maybe the locals will come up with something for us on the night shift."

"I just hope it's not another body," Laura said grimly, getting out of the car. She'd agreed to come back to the motel and get some sleep, but she couldn't help feeling already like it had been the wrong decision. She glanced up at the moon hanging heavy in the sky above her. She'd never seen the appearance of the moon as a reason to quit before. Normally, she and Nate would argue constantly about when it was time to turn in. She always saw it as giving up.

But tonight, it looked like she had no choice but to give up. Nate was already halfway to his room, key in his hand, ready to sleep. Laura sighed and copied him, heading to her own room and unlocking the door before relocking it behind herself. She looked at the bed and for a moment almost couldn't face it. She itched to go back out there and work on the case.

57

But work on what? They had nothing. Unless she was going to go out there and start fingerprinting every single male who walked past her in the center of town, she had nothing to contribute.

Maybe Nate was right. Maybe she just needed some rest.

Laura shrugged off her jacket and kicked off her shoes and then lay down on the bed without getting undressed any further. She needed a minute – a long one. She picked up her phone and found herself scrolling to Chris's name and hitting call, forgetting for a minute about the fact she was supposed to be avoiding him.

Maybe it didn't count if they only talked on the phone. If they didn't see one another, then Laura couldn't witness it happening. If they didn't meet in person, maybe Chris would never meet Zach either.

"Hey," he said, sounding sleepy. "Are you alright?"

"Hi, Chris," Laura said, closing her eyes in the darkness of the room. The only light came from outside, sweeping through the blinds from the parking lot. "Did I wake you?"

"No, but you're just in time," he said. "I was about to turn in. How's your case going?"

"Fine," Laura said, then sighed heavily. "No, sorry, it's going awful. I don't think we're getting anywhere. I feel a bit worn down by it all, to be honest."

"You only just got there last night," Chris said. "Give yourself time. You'll get there. Doesn't it sometimes take months to handle investigations like this?"

"Yes, but…" Laura hesitated. *Yes, but I have psychic visions that mean we usually get these cases solved a lot quicker than most.* "I'm just not used to that."

Chris chuckled. "You mean you're used to being such a great agent that those kinds of timelines don't apply to you," he said. "You better not get too big for your boots, you know. Karma has a way of proving you wrong when you think you're awesome at something."

"Oh, really?" Laura asked. She saw a loose thread and wanted to pick at it, even knowing it might make everything unravel. Part of her wanted to goad him into admitting he wasn't what he seemed. That he was violent. Homicidal. "Has that ever happened to you before?"

Chris got quiet for a minute. "When I first started working with Medicins Sans Frontiers," he said. "I had this thought that I was better than the others. There was a seven-year-old girl. She got hit by shrapnel when her aunt stood on a landmine. When I couldn't save her, that was when I knew I wasn't the hotshot I'd been thinking I was."

Laura's throat went dry. She tried to swallow. "I'm sorry, Chris, I -"

"That's alright," he said, making what sounded like a real effort to cheer up his tone. "Anyway, were you just calling to say hello?"

"Mostly," Laura said. She didn't really know why she'd called. Just that she'd felt down, and her instinct had been to call Chris. That was what was going to make all of this so much harder if her vision did happen. "How's Amy?"

"She's fine. Sleeping already," Chris said. "Talking of the girls, are you coming over this weekend?"

"I don't know," Laura hedged. "I might still be on the case."

"I know that," Chris said breezily. "I get the deal. But we can make plans anyway, can't we? Like normal. If you're still out there Friday, just let me know."

"Yeah," Laura said, her eyes sliding shut for a moment. She didn't know what to say. If she accidentally let it slip that she had been home in time, if that happened... or if Lacey decided to say something about it when she eventually did see Amy again... the lie just wasn't going to work. "Actually, Chris, I don't think we could make it anyway. I just remembered, Lacey has an appointment. Marcus told me one of us has to take her, and if I'm home, I'd like to go with her. But either way, that means we won't be free for the playdate."

"Oh, I see," Chris said. He sounded disappointed, but accepting. "That's a shame. We missed last week as well."

"I know," Laura sighed, doing her best to pretend she was sad about it. It wasn't hard. She *was* sad to have not seen him for so long. It was just that she was also, now, terrified to see him as well. "We'll have to try and make it for the weekend after."

Even as she said the words, she cursed herself. Why bring up the promise of something that she didn't want to happen? But part of her hoped that by the time a couple of weeks had passed, she'd be able to find a way to solve the dilemma of the vision. A way to stop it from happening, maybe. Or maybe she'd have some further details and know that it didn't really mean Chris had a violent maniac lurking just below his surface, like his brother. Anything, really. Anything to put him back as the perfect doctor and humanitarian Laura thought he was.

"What about meeting up without the girls?" Chris asked, making her stomach drop. "I know you don't want to schedule anything this week until you know how you're doing with the case, but what about next Wednesday? Is that far enough ahead?"

"Sure," Laura said, doing her best not to commit to anything. "We'll see how it goes."

There was a brief pause after her words. "Laura, are we okay?" Chris asked. "I'm starting to feel like you don't want to see me."

Laura closed her eyes, mentally shouting at herself. What had she expected? That she could just call him for comfort and then blow him off again, and he wouldn't even notice? "It's not that," she said. "It's just – this job. It's getting to me. And I know I'm always letting you down with scheduling."

"I'm a doctor," he said, stressing his words heavily. "It's honestly a blessing to find someone whose schedule is more unpredictable than mine, because it means I don't have to feel bad about letting *you* down. Trust me. I'm fine with it."

Laura bit her lip. She needed to get out of this conversation now, before she broke down and scheduled a date with him tomorrow and booked a flight there and back so she could stay on the case at the same time. "I know," she said. "I just feel guilty. It's my issue, not yours. But I'll get over it. Look, I should really let you get to bed. I need some rest, too. I've got a long day of work tomorrow."

"Right," Chris said. There was another pause. "Goodnight, Laura."

"Goodnight," Laura said, hanging up the phone and feeling like the worst person in the world.

Except she wasn't, because someone out there was murdering young women, tying them up, and stabbing them to the tune of an old song. And tomorrow, if she did everything she could to stop that person, maybe there was a chance she could redeem herself.

CHAPTER THIRTEEN

Tessa waved one more time and then turned around with a grin on her face, her long legs eating up the road as she walked away from the party.

What a night!

Her head was buzzing, full of the excitement of the evening and the loud music that even now was ringing in her ears. It faded behind her as she walked away but she could still hear it inside – especially the song that had been playing when he kissed her. She could have gone home with him tonight, but that wasn't Tessa's thing. She was careful. She knew even when she was drunk that it wasn't a good idea to go home with someone you'd only just met.

And there was always tomorrow.

Tessa clapped her hands together in front of her as she walked, remembering his number stored in her phone with another grin. Someone who was walking a dog on the other side of the street jumped and looked her way, and Tessa didn't even apologize. She was too giddy. High on the memories already.

It was a long enough walk back home and the night was cold, but Tessa didn't mind. Her bare legs were still fortified by the alcohol, and the boxy jacket she was wearing – stolen from an ex and never returned even after they'd broken up – kept the chill out well enough. She always brought it with her when she knew she'd be leaving a party late in the cold and walking home.

She thought about taking off her shoes and walking barefoot, but discarded the idea. Not until she sobered up enough to actually feel the pain in her feet. She had to keep them on for as long as possible, because you never knew what was littered around on the sidewalk. Broken glass, needles, used chewing gum. Even the euphoria she was feeling from the night wasn't enough to block out that thought, keeping her sensible.

The party faded far behind her and the reality of the night around her began to set in. Tessa held the jacket closer around herself, her arms firmly closed over her chest to keep out any of the chill breeze. She felt like she was walking too fast, maybe about to fall, but she couldn't shut off her momentum fast enough to slow herself down. Besides, the quicker she walked, the quicker she got home. If she could do so before the cold and the pain in her feet started to get to her, so much the better.

The streetlights were almost blinding every time Tessa passed under them, the darkness of the street beyond near perfect. Each time she stepped out of the circle of illumination it felt like she was going to trip over something, totally unable to make out what was coming up next. The houses around were all dark and silent, and Tessa quickened her pace even further until she was almost running. Yes, better to get home sooner rather than later.

She felt like the alcohol was starting to wear off.

She stepped out of the circle of one of the streetlights and almost immediately her momentum caught up with her, making her tangle her feet and drop to the floor with a whoosh of breath. Tessa let out a gasp as she felt her knee hit the sidewalk – definitely not drunk enough anymore to avoid feeling that – and she sat up. There was grit on the palms of her hands where she'd gone down. She tried to brush it off and winced again, realizing it had ground in with her own weight.

Out of nowhere, a hand appeared in front of her.

"Thanks," Tessa said, not even looking up. It was so dark, anyway, and she was still too drunk indeed to be confident about being able to get up on her own. She took the hand and felt it flex and pull, taking her weight as she was yanked to her feet so fast she almost fell again.

There was a blur of movement, confusing and much too fast, and Tessa thought she was going to throw up. She looked ahead. What was that? Wasn't that – wasn't that where she had just come from? Why was she facing the wrong way?

Something pressed against her face – something like a piece of cloth – Tessa squirmed, not wanting it there, but she felt the outline of a hand clamped over her mouth and nose – and there was something behind her holding her still – her hand – he still had hold of her hand – Tessa tried to break free, giving a muffled shout of complaint, trying to get a breath to shout again, a strong chemical smell filling her nostrils –

***

Tessa blinked slowly, trying to open her eyes. They were heavy. Like they had decided they wanted to stay shut. For a moment she wondered if she'd managed to glue her real eyelashes together under the false ones.

Then she managed to get a look at the room she was in, and her confusion deepened.

Wasn't she at home?

She remembered leaving the party, but nothing else. That wasn't too unusual. But – where was she? Normally she managed to find her way home. And this didn't look like someone else's home either. This was – it was like some kind of warehouse. Big and empty. A good venue for a party, actually.

But this wasn't where she had been last night.

Tessa wanted to groan, but she moved her tongue slightly and felt how dry her throat was and held the noise back. She blinked her eyes a few more times to try to clear them. Why did she feel so heavy and slow? How much had she drunk last night?

Had she been spiked?

She turned her head slightly, just a tiny movement, but it sent pain ricocheting through her skull. Hangover. She knew that one well enough. What a time for it to strike, though. Where the hell was she? Was she going to be able to walk home from here, or would she need a cab? And why was she on the floor?

Tessa saw something move ahead of her and realized it was a figure – a person – someone shrouded in so much darkness she hadn't even seen them. "Hey," she croaked, thinking they might be able to tell her where she was and why. She moved to sit up, trying to put her hand down –

And failing.

What the hell?

Tessa moved her hands again and then her feet, realizing in panic that she was tied up. She couldn't move. Not only that, but the figure she had seen had gotten up and was walking towards her – no, not towards her, towards the wall. There was something over there, some kind of box. He did something to it with his back to her and then a song started up, something old and soulful, something she didn't recognize. It didn't sound like it was being played over speakers, either.

He was my man, and we were so happy
Two fools in love, how now it may seem
Now when I think of how I was happy
I don't recall was it nightmare or dream

What was this song? Why was it playing?

To hide her screams?

Tessa stared at him. "Who are you?" she asked. "What are you doing?"

He turned and looked down at her, as if surprised to see her. He had the strangest look on his face. Like he was almost sorry she was down there tied up on her own.

"Allow me to help you up," he said. He reached for her hands and she felt something loosen, and thought he was letting her go. It was weird that she'd been tied up in the first place, but if he was letting her go then she wasn't going to argue. She would just get out of here and go.

He took one of her hands and pulled, and Tessa came right up into his arms, in a standing position. The surprise for a moment took away her concentration, but then she realized. Her feet were still bound at the ankles, making her nearly topple over and lose her balance. And the ropes around her wrists – they were still there, just looser. Loose enough she could move her hands around to her sides, but not much further than that. She tugged at them angrily, wondering what the hell he was playing at.

"Let me go," she snapped, fear making her angry.

"Let's dance first," he said, his voice dreamy, like he wasn't even really there in the room.

That was when Tessa's fear really reached a pitch.

The song continued playing behind them as he slowly began to drag her around, ignoring her bound feet and the fact she couldn't even stumble in a controlled way after him.

He was so fine, I thought I was lucky
A husband, a child, the future I saw
She was this maid from down in Kentucky
Red hair that reached almost down to the floor

Oh, my man and the rose
Oh, how the story goes
Oh, my man and the rose
that took him from me

The man who was holding her stopped moving suddenly, and Tessa looked up into his face, feeling her heart stutter in her chest.

The look on his face was twisted. Furious.

And Tessa knew then she wasn't going to get away from this.

CHAPTER FOURTEEN

Laura rushed forward, trying to stop them from meeting. This was just what she had seen before, and she couldn't let it happen. Not like this.

But it was like her feet were made of lead. Fear made them stick, made them slow, and by the time she had stumbled over to them, Zach and Chris were already deep in conversation.

All she could hear was buzzing in her ears, so loud she couldn't even make out what they were saying. It was happening. It wasn't supposed to happen like this. She'd done everything she could not to let them meet, and now they were meeting anyway. This wasn't right.

She couldn't stop it.

Even as she struggled to grasp the situation, Zach said something that made Chris stop cold, the side of his neck going red. There was a moment when Laura reached out for Chris's arm, trying to hold him back, but she was too slow and her hand closed on air. He was already gone, launching himself at Zach, pushing the old man to the ground. Landing on top of him. Grabbing something out of his pocket – why had he been carrying a knife in his pocket? – and stabbing it into Zach's chest. Laura could only stare and scream as bright red blood surged out of Zach's chest, splattering the pavement, falling back onto his own face as he choked for air…

Laura shot awake to the sound of hammering at the door, sitting bolt upright in bed. She reached for her gun automatically.

"Laura?"

She relaxed, if only by a small amount. That was Nate's voice. Not some crazed attacker – Nate. "What is it?"

"You were screaming. Are you okay?" Nate sounded panicked, like he was about to burst through the door to check for himself.

"Oh, God," Laura muttered, putting a hand against her forehead. She raised her voice again to yell back to him. "Sorry – it was just a dream."

"Jesus." She could almost hear Nate slump against the door in relief. "Well, I just got a call, anyway. The captain's meeting us at a scene in the north of town. They just found another one. It sounds like we're the closest."

Laura glanced at her phone, fully charged beside the bed. It showed two hours until her alarm was due to go off. "I'm coming."

She was actually glad she'd been so tired and stressed out about Chris last night that she hadn't managed to finish getting undressed. She shoved her feet into her shoes, grabbed her jacket and her phone, and yanked open the door, almost beating Nate down the stairs to the car as he locked his motel room door.

She pulled her hair out of its ponytail as she slid into the passenger seat, letting Nate take the wheel. Both of them buckled up and then Nate was driving, screeching right out of the parking lot and onto the road. He was taking turns so quickly on the empty nighttime roads that Laura almost didn't manage to retie her hair into a neat new ponytail before he brought the vehicle to a sudden stop, staring at the GPS. They'd been no more than a couple of minutes away from the scene. Could that possibly be a coincidence, or did the killer know where they were staying?

"I think this is it," he said, peering ahead.

Laura didn't need to confirm it with the GPS. "Let's go!" she said, urgently, opening the door and heading in the direction of the sound she had faintly heard once the engine stopped.

The sound of an old song from the thirties.

It was playing from the building in front of them, some kind of old, abandoned warehouse. It was fenced off, but there was a very obvious man-shaped hole cut through the fencing, and Laura charged through it without a second thought. She drew her gun as she ran, letting her ears guide her. She burst through a door into the warehouse – and there –

Oh, my man and the rose
Oh, how the story goes
Oh, my man and the rose
that took him from me
that took him from me

The last line of the song faded out as Laura rushed to the woman's side, diving to her knees so fast it hurt, almost falling beside her rather than getting down properly. She could see the huge, gaping stab wound in the woman's chest, blood spurting from it – just like it had from Zach in Laura's dream – blood pooling around her on the floor, so much blood…

The woman's eyes were glassy, staring up at the ceiling. Laura touched her neck. She was still warm. She touched a few different spots, hoping she had just missed it, hoping it was faint…

But there was no pulse.

"Laura?" Nate shouted urgently. He was backing into the room, his gun drawn and pointed outwards, breathing heavily.

"We're too late," Laura said, her voice choking in her throat. "She's gone."

Nate moved to her side, though he didn't crouch to her level. Laura looked up at him, tears threatening to spill from her eyes. She'd already touched the girl and there was nothing, no headache. No clues here, either.

"I just ran a quick circuit around the warehouse, looking for him out there," Nate said. "He's long gone. Backup is just pulling up outside. I'm going to organize a search. I'll send someone in here to watch over the scene until forensics can get here."

"He's long gone," Laura said distantly. She felt strangely detached from everything. Like maybe this was still just another dream, even though she knew it was real life. The blood had stopped gushing from the woman's chest. Her heart was done. "Three minutes is a long head start."

"I'm going to try, anyway," Nate said. There was fierce determination in his voice, but when Laura looked up to say something about it, he was gone, too.

She looked down at the dead woman, her eyes looking up and seeing nothing. She had short-cropped black hair, fanned out around her head at the level of her ears. She was pretty. She'd been wearing five sets of earrings in each ear, tiny studs clearly carefully chosen to complement her look. There was black eyeshadow smudged over her eyes. Laura saw every tiny detail, preserved it forever inside her head.

They hadn't been quick enough. Laura had gone to sleep instead of carrying on the search, and because of that, they hadn't been quick enough to stop him from killing her.

She wasn't going to be slow again.

***

Laura watched the sun breaking the rim of the horizon and shielded her eyes, squinting as the first rays shot towards her and glinted off the

67

windows of the police cars. Dawn. About the time she had been thinking she was going to get up.

Well, that had gone out of the window.

"Here," Nate said, coming up beside her with two steaming hot paper cups of coffee in his hands. He passed one over to her. "I found an all-night place not far down the road. One of the detectives took me."

Laura nodded without comment and took a sip, grimacing. It was hot and black, and she figured Nate must have asked for some extra shots judging by the strength. That was fine. It was needed. She'd barely had three hours of sleep, and she knew he must have been somewhere around the same.

"I don't think we're going to get anything at all here," Laura said. "Techs have finished and they said it's the same as last time. They might get some prints, but they'll be useless. We already know his prints aren't in the database."

"I did find the identity of the victim," Nate said. He pulled out his notebook and read from it. "Her name was Tessa Patinson. We have her family address. You want to go visit?"

"Not really," Laura said. She took another hit of the coffee. "But by the time I've finished this, maybe. Let's get over there."

Nate nodded with a smile, a tiny bit of humor in the face of the horror they'd seen. He led the way back to the car and got behind the wheel without asking her if she wanted to drive. Laura was glad. Between the nightmare and now this living nightmare, she wasn't sure she had the concentration left in her to get them there in one piece.

"It's a lot more visceral than I thought," she said, once he was done programming the GPS and they were starting to move out.

"The murder?" Nate asked, throwing a raised eyebrow her way.

"Yeah." Laura slumped in her seat, putting her knees up against the dash. "It's... I don't know. Angrier than I thought. When you see the pictures or even the bodies after they've been cleaned up, it's not the same. But I felt it today. The fury. The rage it would take to really stab someone that deep, to pull the weapon out – whatever it is – and see those great spurts of blood gush right out of the heart. I could understand the first time, but the second and third time – you don't go through with that unless you have a really serious reason to want to."

"It's a serious injury," Nate said, his eyes flicking to his mirrors silently as he drove across the slowly waking town. "I know we haven't found a weapon yet, but I expect it to be a big one. Something that's probably heavy to wield. It's not something you carry around by accident. He knows what he's going to do when he gets started."

"That's part of what worries me," Laura said. "We have three bodies now, but who knows how far this goes? How far he's willing to go?"

Nate grunted. "I don't think we want to know the answer to that."

"There's a message on your phone," Laura said. Nate's cell was lying in the center console between them, and the screen had lit up with an incoming alert.

"It's probably Officer Munson," Nate said. "I found him at the crime scene and asked him to pull me all the information he could find on our victim before we head in to speak to her family. Read it to me?"

Laura pulled the phone out of the console and touched the screen. She turned it towards Nate's face just enough that it would capture his likeness and unlock, without blocking his view of the road, and then opened up the message to read it in full. "Tessa Patinson, twenty-three years old. She lived on her own but her family are local. Family were informed an hour ago and they confirmed they heard from her last night, saying she was going out to a party."

"Do we know if she got there?"

"Nothing that I can see here about it," Laura said. "Anyway, she was a marketing graduate and had just joined a firm to work on their social media and marketing campaigns, and was reportedly settling in well. I don't think I see how there could be a link between her and the other victims, but we can ask."

"Anything about a significant other?" Nate asked.

"Nothing," Laura said. "I don't know if I feel good about this. They're going to be fresh to the grief, and we're going to heap more on them. And I don't even know if I believe we'll find out anything useful."

"Try to stay positive," Nate said. "We have to try. It only takes one clue to break the case."

"I know," Laura said. She sighed heavily, rubbing her forehead. She had a headache, but not from her visions like normal. No, it was just from sheer tiredness.

They were going to have to go through with this. Nate was right. Any stone left unturned was a question mark. But still, Laura wanted to hide under a rock instead of facing this family.

She squared her shoulders as Nate slowed the car to a stop outside a modest family home, feeling like she was about to step into the ring for ten rounds of emotional pummeling.

"Here we go," Nate said.

They got out of the car and moved to the front door, Laura lingering back and allowing Nate to take the lead. He knocked smartly and the door was immediately opened by a detective wearing a badge around his neck. He nodded at them – clearly recognizing them from the precinct, though Laura couldn't recall seeing him herself – and gestured for them to go inside.

"The sister is in the living room," he said, pointing in the right direction.

Laura wondered about where the rest of the family was, following Nate as he entered the room. There was a woman just a little older than Tessa had been sitting on a battered old sofa, and another detective sitting nearby in an armchair. The room was small but furnished well, even if all of the pieces looked a little second-hand. But that wasn't what caught Laura's attention the most when she walked into the room.

What caught her attention the most was a giant portrait of an older man and woman set on the wall above the mantlepiece, printed on canvas. And directly below it, two large silver urns – set with a single candle burning between them.

Ah.

That was why there had been no mention of parents.

"Ms. Patinson?" Nate asked gently, causing the sister to glance up.

"Mrs. Sunter, now," she said, raising what looked like weary eyes. The call had come in during the early hours of the morning. She must have had an unexpected awakening. "Tallie."

"Tallie." Nate sat down next to her but at a respectable distance on the sofa, leaving Laura to find a spot on another armchair set at a right angle to the sofa. "My name is Special Agent Nathaniel Lavoie, and my partner over there is Special Agent Laura Frost. We need to ask you some questions so we can work on finding whoever did this to your sister."

Tallie nodded. There were tear tracks visible on her face, but otherwise she seemed to be holding up well. Her hair was longer than her sister's, and the piercings and smudged black eye makeup weren't there, but the family resemblance was still strong.

"Do you know of anyone who had a reason to dislike Tessa?" Nate asked. "Especially a strong dislike?"

70

Tallie shook her head. "Not specifically," she said. Her voice was raw. "But Tessa got in a bit of trouble from time to time. It's possible there was someone. We just didn't talk much about it."

Nate tilted his head. Laura was sure he was picking up on the same vibe he was. The sister was down here, but not her husband. Tessa had moved out, at a young age, despite not having highly paid work. There were warning signs of a fracture here. "What was your relationship like with Tessa?"

Tallie sighed. "Honestly…" she shook her head. "Lately, it was difficult. She'd moved out last year. After our parents died, I ended up basically having to raise her the rest of the way. Our brothers, too – they're both away at college right now. When I got married, she was the only one still living at home, and she didn't like the way things changed. She told me she felt like my husband forced her out of her own home. We had a few arguments about that. Lately, we were getting back to how it used to be, but we hadn't started talking about the deeper stuff again yet."

Laura groaned internally. That meant they weren't going to get much help from her about anything that would shine a light on Tessa's relationships, her recent movements, or any mention she might have made that could lead them to the killer.

"In that case, I'll just ask this," Nate said. "Do you know of any information that might help us figure out what happened to her last night? However small it may seem?"

Tallie shook her head slowly. "I've been sitting here racking my brain. But I don't know where to start. I don't even know if she was seeing anyone."

This was a waste of time. Laura got up quietly, letting Nate keep the focus of the conversation, and glanced around. There was a shelf full of photographs at one end of the room. She made her way over to it.

"I'm going to give you my card," Nate said, taking one out of his pocket. "If you do happen to think of anything, please don't hesitate to call. Any small lead could make a difference at this stage."

Laura reached out and touched one of the photographs. A picture of Tessa. Maybe one of the few things that remained around here since she'd moved out. It was only a slim hope in the first place, and Laura wasn't even really disappointed when nothing happened. A vision coming from that would have been a lucky shot even when her psychic abilities were firing on all cylinders.

71

"Thank you," Tallie said. "I just feel so awful. My brothers don't even know yet. It's too early in the morning to call them – and they're going to have to find out over the phone, too."

"If you need anything at all, you just talk to these detectives," Nate said, nodding to the local officers who had been left as liaisons by the captain. "They'll give you all the support you need."

That was Laura's cue, as well as Nate's own. He got up and she began moving towards the door already, pre-empting his exit.

He gave Mrs. Sunter one last nod and then turned, with a glance of professional recognition towards the detective remaining in the room, to go.

Laura waited until the front door was closed behind them to speak again, not wanting to be heard by the people inside the house. She glanced back, half-expecting to see the woman's husband framed in the upstairs window, but he wasn't there. She would have been a little interested to find out what the nature of the disagreement was between him and Tessa, but it was something they could circle back to. She wasn't getting the impression they would gain anything from the victims now – and without a link to the other two women, a motive for Tessa's murder meant next to nothing.

"I don't think we're getting anywhere with looking at the victims," Laura said as she got into the car. She turned to Nate in the driver's seat decisively. "Let's come at this from another angle."

"What angle?" Nate asked.

"The song. He wants us to hear it," Laura said. "Every time, he makes sure someone hears it before he leaves. So, let's dive into this song and figure out what he's trying to tell us."

Nate stared the engine with a nod, taking them back to the precinct.

CHAPTER FIFTEEN

Laura swiveled her chair around towards Nate, showing him the results on her phone screen. "I think I've got it," she said.

"That's not fair," Nate complained. "You had way more time than me. This computer's still booting up."

"Don't blame the tools, bad workman," Laura joked, only half-paying attention. "Listen to this. The original singer was Nena Flora, right? It turns out she wasn't even that big of a deal back in the 1930s. She really only had this one hit song. Her Wikipedia page is bare bones – it just has information about this song and not much else. This isn't a song that would be a hugely well-known one even among people who like this kind of music."

"I thought it sounded kind of familiar before," Nate said. "But then, I don't know. Maybe it just has that generic sound that was popular back then."

"That's what I think," Laura agreed. "It was generic. People didn't click with it, for some reason. And the record didn't sell well, so they didn't make a whole lot of copies."

"Really? How many?" Nate asked, turning away from his computer entirely to listen.

"About a thousand." Laura shook her head. "This is a very small amount of records to be out there. I don't know if it's a coincidence that we've seen three of them at crime scenes and one in that antique store already. Maybe we should call him back and ask him if anyone's bought multiple copies of the record."

Nate nodded. "I'll do that in a moment," he said. "Was the singer based around here, or something?"

Laura shook her head. "The record company that released it was based nearby. So, maybe that's why we're able to find more of them in this area. It would make sense. It's possible that it was more of a small, local phenomenon, and no one else ever really heard the record."

"That would be a lot more help if we didn't already guess the killer was from here," Nate said, covering his face with a short bark of a frustrated laugh. "How easy is it to buy?"

"I'll find out," Laura said. "You make that call."

While Nate talked beside her, she tuned him out and focused on her screen. She hit all of the online sales and auction sites she could think of, trying to see how easy it was to find the record to buy. She had a couple of hits – several ended auctions that were still archived, all of them from years ago, and a single current listing. It was rare, but not too valuable, priced around thirty dollars each time. Not a lot, given the rate of inflation since the record was first released.

There was no way to know who had purchased the copies available at auction without getting a subpoena for the records from the auction site, and that would take a long time. But maybe there was another way they could trace the kind of people who bought this record, perhaps even to narrow it down to just one.

"Alright, thanks," Nate said, hanging up the phone. He looked back at Laura. "No luck. He says that copy we saw was donated from a house clearance after an elderly local resident passed away. He's had it for years and it never sold. He's never seen another copy."

"Alright," Laura said. "Well, I have another idea. This is so rare that it really seems like it would only be of interest to collectors – people who like to own rare things for the sake of saying that they do."

"That makes sense," Nate nodded. "Did you find any?"

"I found some listings online, but only a few, and years old," she said. "I'm thinking we make some calls and try to find out who the big record collectors are around here."

"Where do we even start?" Nate asked with a frown. "Is there... I don't know, some kind of forum for this?"

"Only one way to find out," Laura said, nodding towards his computer screen.

Nate turned and typed into his search engine, looking for results connected to the song title and singer name along with various keywords that might lead them to a buyer. Finally, he got a hit – an online trading forum where serious record collectors could discuss their finds.

"Right," he said, reading out loud from the screen. "This guy, MDColl59, posted that he wants a copy of the record and asked if anyone had seen it around. He gets a whole load of nothing in the replies. There's even one other poster who says, 'I'm not helping you out after the way you've treated people around here.'"

"That sounds juicy," Laura said. "Let's do a search for MDColl59 and see what comes up."

Nate did as he was told, studying the results carefully. "Here, hang on. It looks like another thread on the same forum telling people to stay away from this collector."

Laura scooted her chair forward to get a look at the screen herself, wanting to read it. "What are they saying?"

"Uh, let's see – this one says he was swiped at the last minute when the collector followed him and bid higher on the record collection that he wanted," he said. "Another one said it doesn't surprise him, MD pushed him to the floor when they were at an estate sale so he could get the chance to bid. And this one says he's too much of a shark to compete with, he just leaves whenever he sees him enter an auction. And – aha!" Nate laughed, making Laura scan the screen urgently, trying to figure out what he'd seen.

"What is it?"

"Well, then MDColl59 himself found the thread and said they were all a bunch of – well, I'll not repeat the language," Nate chuckled. "Looks like the thread was locked by a moderator after that."

Laura smirked, but it wasn't really that funny – after all, this man was potentially a killer. He'd clearly demonstrated violent tendencies and wasn't afraid to trample over others to get his way. Maybe they had a good shot here.

"Now, we just need to find out who he is," Laura said.

"No need to try too hard," Nate said. "Here's another post. He's asking for a forum member to send him something in the mail, and he's given his name and address. He's a local."

Laura hit the desk in excitement – perhaps too hard, given how many people around them turned to stare at her. "This has to be it," she said. "Let's go and get him."

"Hold on a minute," Nate said, shaking his head in amusement. "Don't forget we have to actually do due diligence. And we might want to think about a search warrant, if we're serious about this guy."

"Look him up on the system," Laura urged.

Nate turned to type, paused, and then shook his head. "No results. He's never been arrested."

"Well, then, there you go!" Laura exclaimed. "We know our suspect must not be in the system, because we don't have his fingerprints. Come on, let's just go and talk to him. I don't want to wait."

"Why not?" Nate asked. "We might as well do it right."

"No, but this killer strikes during the day as well as the night," Laura argued. "If we delay going over there, he might take someone else. We can't let that happen."

Nate sighed and rubbed his face. "Fine. Just let me tell the captain we're on the way so he can send backup if we need them to, and we'll go. But remember what I said before, Laura. No heroics."

"We're just going to talk to him," Laura smiled innocently. "And if he's got nothing to hide, I'm sure he'll be fine with coming over to the precinct for a little more in-depth of a chat."

Nate shook his head and strode off.

"See you at the car!" Laura called after him, grabbing the keys from his desk.

CHAPTER SIXTEEN

Laura almost leapt out of the car as Nate rolled to a stop – until his heavy "No!" stopped her in her tracks.

"What is it?" she asked, glancing around, looking for the hazard that had made him call out to her.

"Let me go first," Nate said grumpily. He really was overreacting to this whole thing. Laura had been injured a few times in the line of duty – so what? It had never been really serious. And the only reason why it happened was because she cared so much about following her visions and making sure that no one died. She was cautious most of the rest of the time.

Laura let Nate get out of the car with a roll of her eyes and then followed him up to the front door of the small but nicely kept home. There was a neat front yard flowering with rose bushes that appeared to be well-tended, and when Nate knocked, they heard a woman's voice merrily calling out to tell them she'd only be a moment.

The door opened a moment later as promised, and Laura had to blink. The person who had answered the door was a little old woman, white-haired but dressed immaculately in matching pink clothes and with a cheerful smile on her face.

"Hello, dears," she said. "What can I do for you?"

"Um, hi," Laura said, taking over from a completely startled Nate. "We're looking for a collector of vintage records. His name is Frank or Frankie Davidson."

"Francesca," she said, looking between them expectantly. "Do you have a lead on a record for me?"

Laura blinked. She looked up at Nate, who was doing the same.

"Sorry," she said. "Are you MDColl59?"

"That's right, dear," she smiled benevolently. "Now, do you want to come in? I can make you some tea."

"Sure," Nate said, though he gave Laura an utterly bewildered look as the woman turned to lead them inside the house.

Laura could only shrug and gesture for him to follow her.

"Now, do you take milk or sugar?" Frankie asked, leading them into a sitting room that was utterly dedicated to records. All four walls were lined, wherever possible, with square shelving units, floor to ceiling. Inside each of those squares were maybe twenty-five or thirty records in their sleeves, and all of them were full.

"Actually, I'd rather talk about the records," Laura said, sensing a need for a change in subject before they ended up sitting around eating cake and making small talk. "You're quite the collector, it looks like."

Frankie looked around and nodded with a small smile of pride. "Yes, I have dedicated an awful lot of time to it," she said with a kind of girlish grin. "I never married or had children, you see. All of the money I earned in my life is mine to spend on myself. And this is what I do with it."

Laura's head was reeling. She took a seat on a sofa that was covered by a knitted blanket with record shapes sewn into it, Nate sitting by her as Frankie arranged herself primly in an armchair. She felt like she was on the back foot. She'd come here expecting to arrest a killer, and instead found a little old lady who couldn't possibly be the person they were looking for.

"You have quite a reputation in the collecting world," Nate said cautiously.

Frankie laughed merrily. "Oh, that! You didn't actually believe anything you read online, did you?" She gestured towards a computer sitting on a small desk in the corner. "We do have fun. We make all the new collectors think I'm some sort of shark so they won't go after the best hauls. We've been doing it for years. Occasionally, someone catches on, and then they become one of us, so to speak."

"Do you know of anyone who was looking for copies of a particular record?" Laura asked, deciding to just throw it out there. "The singer was Nena Flora, and the song was -"

"My Man and the Rose," Frankie said. She nodded. At Laura's sharp look, she gave a movement of dismissal. "I have a photographic memory, so I remember every record I've ever seen. That one doesn't appear much, though."

"Do you have a copy yourself?"

Frankie screwed up her nose and shook her head. "Heavens, no. What would I do with such a thing? It would just be taking up space."

"But you posted on the forums asking for information about where to get one," Laura said, frowning.

Frankie paused for a moment, then laughed. "Oh, yes! I remember. Another little one of our forum jokes. It's funny because the record is just worthless. It's the kind of thing an amateur would go for, just because there aren't many of them around."

"That doesn't make it valuable?" Laura asked.

"Let me put it this way," Frankie said, folding her hands in her lap. "There are some books which are not discovered during the lifetime of the author, and then later on, they are discovered and become incredibly popular. Then, first editions become extremely valuable. On the other hand, there are some books which don't sell well because they are simply not very good, and those books don't ever become valuable at all. They sink into obscurity and no one even recalls the name of the author. A hundred years later, the book may as well never have been written. It's the same with art. For every van Gogh, there are perhaps hundreds of painters we've never heard of, because they never had any real talent. And when it comes to records, there are also certain songs which need never have seen the light of day."

"So, you've never heard of a collector actually genuinely wanting this particular record for their collection?" Nate asked. Laura was still blinking a little, impressed by Frankie's way with words in crafting the analogy.

"I can't say I have," Frankie said. She looked at Laura with a sort of tilted expression, as though she was looking over a pair of spectacles – though she wasn't wearing any. "Would you like some tea, now?"

"I think we'd better keep moving," Laura said with a polite smile. "Actually, if you wouldn't mind – would it be possible for us to have a little look around at your collection?"

"To make sure I'm telling the truth, you mean?" Frankie asked. "Dear, I have thousands of records here. Some of them are in picture sleeves. You're welcome to look, but I would imagine it will take hours."

Laura nodded. There was such a thing as doing due diligence – but then there was also such a thing as being realistic. Frankie hadn't killed anyone. How could she? She was a tiny old lady. That didn't mean she couldn't have a co-conspirator, but then again, owning the record wouldn't make her a killer, either.

"Where were you yesterday?" she asked, just to have an alibi they could check, just in case.

"Bridge club," Frankie shot back immediately. "Followed by a rather stirring auction in the next town over. I didn't manage to buy anything – I was outbid a fair few times. But you could talk to the auctioneer. I'm sure he'd remember me. After that, I had dinner with a friend and retired back here to bed."

It was comprehensive, as far as an alibi went. It sounded like her whole day was accounted for. Like she had a busier social life than Laura did. In fairness, that wasn't difficult.

"I'm sorry to have taken up your time," Laura said, knowing it was time to wrap things up. "If you do happen to hear of anyone who is buying up copies of this record, you'll let us know, won't you? It sounds like it would be an unusual event."

"Of course," Frankie said, refolding her hands in her lap. "I think I might try and buy a few myself."

"You just said it was worthless," Nate said, standing up ready to leave as Laura did the same.

"It is," Frankie said, with a cunning twinkle in her eye. "But if the FBI are asking me about that record in particular, then I think the smart move might be to get a few extra copies in case the price goes up sometime soon."

"I won't comment on that," Nate said, with the particular roguish grin that usually seemed to make him a favorite of older women.

They walked to the door with Frankie's laughter ringing out behind them, and Laura found herself seizing onto a new determination despite the disappointment.

Frankie Davidson wasn't their killer. In fact, she wasn't even close. But she'd given them something to think about – and, Laura thought now, a new direction that might just give them the answers they were looking for.

CHAPTER SEVENTEEN

He was walking down the hall, squeak of shoe soles on polished floors, trying not to feel sickened by that smell that always seemed to be everywhere here. Cleaning fluid. Medicine. Something far too sterile to be nice. Maybe it was the knowledge that the cleaning was done to take care of vomit and blood and other bodily fluids, and the kind of germs that could kill.

He was just reaching the doors of the ward when he heard someone call his name from the side, and looked up to see his grandmother's doctor flagging him down.

"Hey," the doctor said when he caught up to him. "I was waiting for you to come in. You're on your way for a visit?"

He nodded. His fingers clutched tighter around the handle of the plastic bag full of treats that he'd brought for her. Magazines and books and some of the foods she was allowed to eat.

"Can we take a moment to talk before you go in?" the doctor asked. "We have some results to discuss."

He nodded. "Okay." There was a pit in his stomach that had started when the doctor called out for him, and it was growing wider by the second.

"Alright, follow me," the doctor said, turning on his heel and heading to the left, away from the ward. He hurried to keep up. They dodged past nurses and through doorways and around stations, until he was totally lost. He was never going to find his way back to the ward alone. Finally, the doctor stopped outside a door, pushed in a keycode, and opened it, leading him into an office.

"Is it serious?" he asked. There was a reasonable basis for the assumption. He guessed the doctor didn't take people into his office to tell them that everything had come back fine.

"I'm afraid it is," the doctor said, sitting and smoothing down his tie. He gestured to a chair in front of the desk. "Please, sit down."

He sat; he waited.

"From the tests we've been conducting, we've built up quite a picture of your grandmother's mental health," the doctor said. "I'm afraid it's not good news. I suspect that she suffers from a form of undiagnosed schizophrenia; she would have benefited greatly from treatment earlier in life, but unfortunately it wasn't caught until now."

There was a pause, like the doctor was giving him a chance to digest the news. "Okay," he said.

"The reason I say I suspect it, rather than being able to give you a diagnosis, is that there's a complication," the doctor said. "Your grandmother also has early stage dementia. Unfortunately, there's no way to reverse the damage that has already been done or to stop it from spreading. Frankly speaking, the prognosis is not good."

He nodded slowly. Inside, though, he was wondering where this doctor got his medical degree from. Didn't they have to go through checks to make sure they were suitable for employment at the hospital? Wasn't this a reputable kind of place?

"I'll give you some leaflets which tell you about your options," the doctor said, reaching for a stack on his desk and passing them across. He took them mechanically, even though he knew he didn't need them. "I do need you to understand that, sooner rather than later, your grandmother is going to be incapable of making her own decisions. You're going to need to start making them for her."

"Right," he said, nodding. He put the leaflets into the plastic bag with a rustle. He could throw them away when he got home. He just had to try to make sure he remembered not to hand them over to her when he saw her in a moment. He stood up from the chair. "I'll go see her now."

The doctor frowned at him slightly. "I think that's a good idea," he said. "But do make sure you read up on those leaflets. They'll tell you everything you need to know."

"I will," he promised, which was a lie. There was just no need.

He was already doing everything he could to save her. The leaflets would be useless once she was healed. Once she was back to normal. It would all be over then, and she would come home, and they would live the way they always had.

He walked back to the ward by some miracle and then to the room he already knew well, the room where she'd been staying all week. It was a shared room, but that was fine. The other residents on the ward spent most of their time asleep. And besides, it gave them something to giggle about together.

"Hi," he said, approaching her bed with a smile. He was hesitant inside, but he didn't let it show on his face. He knew she hated it when he was hesitant and shy and nervous. She would tell him to grow a spine or get out of her sight.

"Hello," she beamed, sitting up a little straighter in the bed. "You're here at last. I thought you weren't coming."

"I just got a little held up," he said, leaning down to kiss her on the cheek. She didn't need to know what he was held up by. "I brought you some snacks."

"Did you get those cookies I wanted?" she asked eagerly, almost like a little girl.

"I did," he said, grabbing them out of the bag with a rustle. He put them down onto her bedside tray and wheeled it over to her so she could reach them.

"Well, then, let's have cookies and talk about your day," she said, smiling as she opened the packet for them. He sat down in the chair beside her and took a cookie first, chewing it while he thought about what he was going to say.

"Nothing much happened today," he said at last. "I just went to the store for you and came here."

"Well, then let's have a good hour or so to make up for it," she said, biting into one of the cookies herself. She reached out and tapped his hand on the bedsheet, then held it, keeping him there. Warmth spread through him from her touch. She was still his grandmother. Despite what any of the doctors could say, she was still always going to be that. He would make sure of it.

"These are good," he offered, finishing his cookie, and dusting off his spare hand on the side of his jeans.

"Did you hear anything about school?" his grandmother asked. "Have they given you the extension you asked for?"

"I've been working on it this morning," he said. "I'm still doing the work until I hear back from them. It shouldn't be too long now. Maybe tomorrow or the day after."

His grandmother snatched her hand back out of his with a furious look. "So you *did* do something today!"

"Only studying," he said. "I didn't think it was worth mentioning."

"You lied to me," she hissed. The woman in the next bed over stirred slightly. He shook his head, swallowing.

"I didn't mean to," he said. "I really didn't think you meant studying. I thought you meant, you know, going out and doing things. That's all."

"You're trying to gaslight me," she snapped. "That's what you're doing. You're going to make me think I'm losing my mind. Well, I'm not, you know. So you can tell those doctors to stop being part of the act as well!"

"I'm not trying anything," he pleaded.

"Don't you talk back to me, boy!" she snapped, her eyes flashing anger. She lifted her hand into the air and he backed away, almost knocking his chair over in his haste to move backwards. "Where are you going?"

"S-sorry," he said. "I've got to go. I've got some things to do. I'll be back tomorrow."

He turned and fled before she could yell at him again, and still her voice echoed after him as he escaped the ward.

He had to finish his work. That was the only way to save her.

He had to finish his work now.

CHAPTER EIGHTEEN

Laura was already typing things into her cell phone as Nate drove, following the rabbit hole where it would take her. She started with a search for Nena Flora, trying to find out exactly who the singer had been – beyond the barren Wikipedia page.

When you couldn't find out what you needed to about a celebrity, you just had to treat them like a normal citizen. Laura searched birth and marriage records, trying to find a mention of the name.

"Here we are," she exclaimed. "Nena Flora lived here in the area in the 1930s. That must be why she worked with this particular record company. She was a local."

"Did she have any kids?" Nate asked.

Laura's lips curved up at the edges. He was always thinking along exactly the same lines she did. It was why they were so good at working together. She had already figured that a child of the singer would have a deep personal connection to the song – a song that no one else knew about. They would even have a deep personal reason to want to make it famous again. If they were already inclined towards killing, maybe it would make a twisted sense to incorporate the song. "I've got two children registered in the late thirties. Then those two kids also have children registered – I'm seeing one in the fifties and one in the sixties. They each just had one child."

"And those descendants?"

"Nothing registered locally for the first one," Laura said. "I'm just looking… ah, here we go. One more Flora born in 1992. He was registered at the local hospital."

"He'd still be alive, not to mention fit and healthy," Nate pointed out. "Even the father could be a potential, if they're still fit."

"No, I have a death record here," she said. "But the son is alive, from what I can tell."

"Put a call in to the precinct," Nate suggested. "Get his current address."

Laura put the phone to her ear and dialed, waiting tensely.

"Hello, you've reached -"

"Hi," Laura said, cutting them off. "This is Special Agent Frost. I need an address check on a Jack Flora."

"Give me one second." There was a pause. "Alright, I do have an address for that individual. It's downtown. Would you like me to read it out to you?"

"Yes, go ahead," Laura said, her hand hovering over the touchscreen for the GPS, ready to put it in. She moved her hands over the screen rapidly to keep up, then thanked the officer when the address was finished and ended the call.

"Fifteen minutes from here," Nate said. "Shall we?"

"It would be rude not to," Laura grinned.

One setback, but then one step forward. Maybe they were actually getting closer this time. If they were about to find the killer, Laura knew she'd rest easy tonight – impending vision of doom or not. Because this was starting to feel like one of those cases that may end up never getting solved.

Nate put the car into drive, and Laura tried to think of all the ways she could lead this man into admitting he was a killer – so they could get this over with sooner rather than later.

***

The door opened so quickly that Laura was actually surprised, but not as much as the man who opened it. He looked them up and down with a frown. "Where's my pizza?" he asked.

"We're not delivery drivers," Laura said with a wry smile. "I take it you're expecting a late lunch."

"Early dinner," he replied. "Who are you, then?"

Laura and Nate both took their badges out of their pockets without a word.

"What?" he said, looking at them and blinking. "I haven't done anything wrong!"

"That's very defensive, considering we haven't accused you of anything," Laura said evenly. "We wanted to speak with you about your great-grandmother, Nena Flores."

He tilted his head with a scrunched-up expression. "Why?"

"I think we're better off discussing that inside," Laura said, gesturing for him to lead the way.

He stepped back reluctantly, clearly not wanting to let them in but having very little choice. Once they were inside, he lead them to the

86

first room they came to, which contained a sofa, TV, and not much else. This was a small home, but clearly he was finding it difficult to furnish even that much space.

"I don't know a whole lot about Nena," he said, before they'd even finished sitting down. Nate stood in front of the sofa awkwardly, having no space to sit. "It's just a part of my family history that no one ever really talked about. I mean, I haven't even thought about her in years, to be honest."

"Really?" Laura asked. "Even though she was an accomplished singer?"

"I wouldn't say accomplished," Jack said, wrinkling his nose. "She had one song. It's more of an interesting fact I can trot out at parties than anything else. Most people haven't ever heard of it."

"You didn't feel proud of that part of your heritage?" Nate pressed.

Jack snorted. "Heritage? It's not really anything to do with me. My great-grandma recorded a song, so what? It's not like anyone really heard it. It was a flop. She never even made any money off it."

"There were no royalties?" Laura asked.

"From a song no one bothered listening to?" Jack said. "Please. She died penniless. She had nothing. We all had nothing. My father ended up dragging himself up out of that. Not that I'm much better off myself, these days."

Laura frowned to herself. She knew the song hadn't been so successful, but it was odd to think that the singer hadn't made any other successes either. "She didn't record anything else?"

"The record company wouldn't let her," Jack shrugged. "The family lore is that she wanted to sing her own songs and they wouldn't let her. They said she had to sing this one first, and then it flopped, so they cut her loose. Some legacy to be proud of, right? She had one chance and it wasn't even one of her own songs."

"So, she didn't write it," Laura said. This was getting more complex than she'd thought. Not only was there clearly no love lost for Jack's memory of his great-grandmother, but now there were more people involved in the making of the song than she'd thought.

"No, it was some other woman's song. You know, she was sad about that. When she was dying, she told my dad – my grandad was gone by then, he got hooked on drugs – that it was her biggest regret in life. She said she had no connection to the song, you know? She didn't feel it. That's what you can hear on the record. She just doesn't care enough about the words, so you don't care enough."

87

Laura rubbed her forehead. "So, who did have a personal connection to the song?"

Jack shrugged. "Beats me. I didn't ever look into it. Like I said, it wasn't something we talked about much. It haunted her, I think. When that happens, your children don't want to keep bringing it up. I think if she had her way, I would never have even heard of the song at all."

This was so curious. For a singer to be actually ashamed of the only song they ever got a chance to release… that didn't tally, somehow, with Laura's impression of the crime scenes. Yes, on paper, it would be logical to think that this man could blame the song for ruining his great-grandmother's life, and the effects of that trickling down to ruin his own. But there was something about it that seemed off with her. The killer *wanted* them to hear the song. Almost like he was proud of it or loved hearing it.

"Can you tell us your whereabouts last night?" Nate asked. "Or, no, this is easier – two days ago, during the day?"

"I was at work," he said. "I'm a shift worker at one of the factories on the outskirts of town. Today's my day off. We've been doing fourteen, fifteen-hour shifts."

"Fifteen hours?" Nate repeated.

"I mean." Jack's eyes slid to the side. "Ten hours. That's right. We had a three-hour break so I got confused."

Alright, Laura thought. *Clearly, someone at that factory is breaking labor laws.*

But that wasn't what they were here for, so she let it pass.

"If we were to check with your foreman, they would have timesheets?" Laura asked. There was probably surveillance footage as well, of course, and they could collect witness statements. But it didn't hurt to give a little push, just in case the alibi was a fake and they would want to admit it when they realized it was going to be tested.

"Yeah," Jack shrugged. "I was there all day. We do three days in a row, take a break, and then three more. I was there yesterday all day as well, and the day before the one you're asking about."

If he was telling the truth, he was ruled out of at least two of the murders on timing grounds. He could still have committed the one last night, but after a fifteen hour shift at work? It was doubtful he would have had the energy.

"Alright," Laura said. "Thank you for your help. You don't happen to have any documents from around that time pertaining to the song…?"

Jack shook his head. "From what I hear, I think Nena would probably have burned them all in disgust."

Laura sighed and nodded, looking at Nate. "Then we'll be on our way." To where, though, she had no idea – because she was completely out of leads, and the killer was still out there, what might as well have been a thousand miles away for how close they were to catching him.

CHAPTER NINETEEN

Laura slumped in the car, holding her hand against her head.

"We'll get there," Nate said.

"It doesn't feel that way right now," Laura replied, her voice muffled by her own hand.

"We will," Nate said. Laura had no idea how he was holding onto his determination right now, but she was glad. At least one of them still felt like this case was solvable.

Her phone rang in her hand and she glanced at the screen. Zach. There was no way she was answering it right now. Not with Nate right next to her in the car, and not while she felt like a total failure. She canceled the call, turning the phone over so she didn't have to look at it. She'd call him back soon. Maybe.

Maybe not.

"Who was that?" Nate asked, glancing at her.

"Didn't recognize the number," Laura lied, staring out of the window. He was driving them back to the precinct. She didn't really know why or what they were going to do when they got there.

Her phone buzzed again. Laura couldn't believe it. Was he harassing her or something? She turned it over to reject the call a second time – but stopped with her finger hovering over the button, saving herself before she pressed it. She put the phone to her ear and accepted the call, clearing her throat.

"Special Agent Laura Frost," she said.

"Frost, it's Chief Rondelle," he said, which she knew, because of the caller ID. "How are you getting on with the case?"

Laura closed her eyes momentarily. If he was in as bad a mood now as he had been before they left, she was about to get it with both barrels. "We're still chasing down leads, sir."

Nate glanced at her sideways. He must have been able to just about hear Rondelle's tinny voice from the speakers.

"Still? You don't have any results yet?" Rondelle snapped. Laura groaned inwardly. He *was* in a bad mood.

"We've been able to rule out a few suspects so far," Laura said. "We're getting closer. We have a new lead which we're following right now which feels very promising."

It was a lie, but she hoped it would get him off their case.

"What lead is that?" Rondelle asked.

"Um," Laura said.

Rondelle didn't wait for her to recover. "Look, I've got a report on my desk here that there's been a third murder, and the press are going wild," he said. "You don't get this solved quickly and it's going to be a damn circus."

"I know, sir," Laura said. She cleared her throat. "Oh, we're just pulling up to interview our next suspect. I have to go. We'll let you know as soon as we have some good progress!"

"See that you do," Rondelle replied grumpily, just before she hung up the phone.

She sighed, slumping back into her seat and groaning.

"That's going to backfire if we really can't think of a new lead," Nate said mildly.

Laura stared at him. "You don't think we're going to be able to find a new lead? You just said -"

"I wholeheartedly believe in us and our skills," he said. "I was just saying, lying might not have been the smart thing to do."

"It wasn't your ear he was shouting into," Laura muttered.

She rubbed her forehead again, trying to think. She needed a vision. A vision of the case – not another of the frustrating and terrifying visions of Chris and Zach. Something that would tell her which direction to go in. Anything would help. Anything would be better than their current directionless status.

"We're nearly back," Nate said. "What do you want to look at next? We could go back over ourselves and do that interview with the family of the first victim we never got around to? Check out the first crime scene?"

Laura shook her head slowly. There didn't seem to be any point. But they needed to do *something*.

Her phone buzzed again, and Laura felt like she was going mad.

She flipped it over and her heart skipped a beat, her hand hesitating above the screen, unsure of what to do. It was Chris, this time. She checked the clock on the dashboard – he must have just left work. Maybe that was why the calls were all happening at once – maybe Rondelle was just about to leave his desk, though Laura would believe that when she saw it. And maybe Zach had some kind of false impression that FBI agents clocked off at the same time as everyone else.

She wanted to talk to Chris. She didn't want to talk to Chris with Nate sitting right next to her and listening in. She wanted to make sure that Chris thought they were okay so it didn't ruin whatever budding relationship they had, even if she didn't feel okay right now. She didn't want to have to face up to the vision again.

Laura rejected the call.

"Another unknown number?" Nate asked, with an amused glance in her direction.

"Keep your eyes on the road," Laura muttered.

"Seriously," Nate said. "What's going on? Are you avoiding someone at home?"

"I'm just not in the right frame of mind to talk right now," Laura said. "I'm likely to snap someone's head off because of the case."

"I agree with that," Nate said, in a tone that suggested she had already snapped off his. "But is that all it is? You've seemed a little off since we started this case."

Laura shook her head and looked out of the window so he wouldn't be able to see her expression. "That's all it is."

She was well aware that she was doing it again. Keeping secrets from him. It had almost cost them any kind of relationship once before. Now that he knew about her psychic powers, he held her life and reputation in his hands – he could easily try to out her. Not that anyone would believe him, but Laura didn't want to have to defend herself and lie even more.

And yet, she couldn't bring herself to talk about the vision of Chris stabbing Zach. About how she was avoiding them. Better to let him think she was just having an argument with Chris or something, which was what Laura would have assumed if Nate was rejecting calls from his girlfriend. And better to let him assume rather than saying the lie outright.

She didn't know what to do about all of it. Nate was pulling into the precinct and Laura felt like she would rather have been going anywhere else in the world – anywhere she didn't have to think about this stupid case.

Not even the singer who'd sung it wanted to think about the damn song anymore, and that just about summed the whole thing up.

Laura sat up in her seat. "I've got an idea," she said, her words rushing out in one go, full of excitement.

"Really?" Nate asked, pulling into the precinct parking lot. "About the case?"

"Yes," Laura said, full of a new determination, getting her second wind. "I know who we need to look into next."

CHAPTER TWENTY

"Okay," Laura said, leading Nate down the stairs towards the basement. "So. We know that the victims don't really mean much, right? There's no link between them that we can see. In terms of the case, they're basically useless to us."

"Right," Nate said, though he sounded a little uncomfortable declaring the victims to be useless.

"So, what does that leave? We've got the crime scene, with its careful staging, the method of murder, and…"

"The song," Nate said. "That's why we talked to that Jack Flora guy just now. It didn't get us anywhere."

"But it's not just a clue about the song, is it?" Laura said. They pushed their way through the doors to the evidence room. "He could have just left us a copy of the record to find. Or played it on an MP3 device – you can get those cheaper than you can gramophones. Something about us *listening* to the song is important."

"So, what's your idea?" Nate asked.

"My idea is to listen to the song," Laura said. She leaned on the desk, smiling at the officer in charge of the evidence locker. "Hi. Can we go in and play one of the records on one of the gramophones?"

"Sure," he said, passing her the register to sign. "Might be nice to have some music in here."

"The music that was played over the corpse of several young women as they lay dead from a stab wound?" Nate asked, with a raised eyebrow.

Laura shook her head at him and rolled her eyes. "Stop ruining the man's day," she told him, heading for the cage that contained all the evidence. She felt excited, almost giddy. This was something. She knew this was something.

"Here we go," she said, walking over to one of the gramophones which had been stacked in the corner. She carefully put on a pair of gloves, as she knew she would be expected to, and set the gramophone up to play. Maybe hearing the music, feeling the vibration of it from close by, would be enough to set off a vision. She set it going and then rested, leaning on the table to get as much contact with the music as she could, and listened.

He was my man, and we were so happy
Two fools in love, how now it may seem
Now when I think of how I was happy
I don't recall was it nightmare or dream

Laura grabbed her notebook out of her pocket and uncapped her pen, starting to write the lyrics down as she heard them. The start of the song was kind of generic, in terms of the storyline. A song about a broken relationship. That was pretty normal for music from all time periods, wasn't it?

She came along, with a rose in her hair
Pretty and young, with a smile like sunshine
How could I know that he'd put it there?
Or that she'd taken the man that was mine?

Laura looked at the lines she'd written down. Pretty and young – didn't that kind of sound like all three of the victims? Even though they were actually different ages, they weren't old. And they were all pretty women. Then again, maybe that was just a coincidence.

He was so fine, I thought I was lucky
A husband, a child, the future I saw
She was this maid from down in Kentucky
Red hair that reached almost down to the floor

Red hair... that made her think about Jenna James. She'd been so beautiful, even in death. That beautiful red hair fanned out around her face. It didn't reach to the floor, of course, but she did have a lot of it. Red hair... could that mean something?

Oh, my man and the rose
Oh, how the story goes
Oh, my man and the rose
that took him from me

It was late at night when I saw them both

95

Leaving that bar with his jacket on her
I couldn't believe it, yes I was loath
To think that coat was a gift from my sir

Laura paused on that line. Jacket... she remembered how at one of the crime scenes, a coat had been discarded in the corner. Was that relevant? Or was she just looking for sense where there really was none?

He kept her warm while my heart grew colder
Their fingers entwined while mine, they were numb
Since that night even though I grow older
I can't understand how I was so dumb

They were on the bridge, their breath was misting
When I looked up and saw them both up there
My watch, it stopped when I saw them kissing
My man and the girl with the rose in her hair

Oh, my man and the rose
Oh, how the story goes
Oh, my man and the rose
that took him from me

The last line faded out, the music giving a final slow flourish and then a sad note to end the song. The record rotated on silently a few more times before Laura reached out to turn the gramophone off. It was no less haunting here in an evidence locker than it had been out there at the crime scenes. The song was generic, though, she could hear that now. There wasn't enough feeling in the woman's voice. She maintained that husky tone, never breaking or wavering. It was the music behind the vocal that conveyed all of the emotion.

Still, there was something here. There had to be. Laura looked over what she had written again, thinking. Nate stood silently next to her — whether he was thinking his own thoughts or just giving her space, she didn't know, and she didn't ask. She focused on the words.

The jacket line stood out to her each time she passed over it, like a thorn in an otherwise smooth rose stem. The jacket.

"Crime scene photos." Laura looked at Nate. "Do we have them all yet? Including the last one?"

"I'll grab them from upstairs," Nate replied, moving quickly. He left Laura alone for a while, going over the song. *Red hair. Jacket. Rose in her hair. Smile like sunshine. Pretty and young.* Those were all the descriptions given of the song's antagonist – the woman who had stolen the vocalist's man. There was something here, a conviction growing inside of Laura. A thought that refused to go away, nagging at her each new time she read the lyrics.

"Hey," Nate said, coming from the front of the cage again. He must have almost run up there and back – that, or Laura was more lost in thought than she had realized. "Got them."

"Thanks," Laura said, absent-mindedly, already taking them from his hands and beginning to spread them out in front of herself on the floor. She stood above them, looking down, getting a full picture of each of the scenes.

She frowned, crouching next to the final set of images, and Nate joined her.

"Here," she said, pointing to the photograph of Tessa Patinson lying on her back. "Does that look like a man's jacket to you?"

Nate studied it for a moment. "Yes, I'd say so. Looks like a partner slipped it around her when she was cold. But then again, maybe she just likes the boxy cut."

"It's a man's jacket." Laura had conviction now. "Here, Jenna Janes – she had red hair."

"Right," Nate said. He sounded like he wondered where she was going with this, but he would let her get there.

"And here," Laura added, pointing at the second victim – Dakota Henson. "That headband she's wearing. It looks like a rose, doesn't it?"

Nate shrugged. "I'm not a flower expert, but sure."

Laura's heart was racing in her chest.

This was it.

"Oh, Jesus," she said, staring down at these woman and shaking her head in horror.

"What?" Nate asked, on instant alert.

"I know how he's choosing them," she said. She covered her mouth for a moment, the full implications setting in. Of how unlucky these women had been. How something so innocent had lost them their lives. "They represent the lyrics of the song."

"Are you sure?" Nate asked, scrambling to look at her notes and compare them to the photographs.

Laura no longer needed the notes. She had read them enough times that for the short term, at least, she had them memorized. "Listen. 'She came along, with a rose in her hair, Pretty and young, with a smile like sunshine.' Pretty and young could be all of them, and if they were smiling while they walked along the road, that's it. Anything could have made them smile. A message from a friend. Seeing a cute dog. Who knows what – even just smiling at a stranger. And Dakota Henson was wearing a rose in her hair."

"And then Jenna Janes is the next verse," Nate said, catching on as he read it out from her notebook. "' Red hair that reached almost down to the floor'. Though I don't know if she's from Kentucky."

"She wouldn't need to be – I think he's doing this visually," Laura said. "He sees someone on the side of the road, walking down the street, who looks like she belongs in the song. Then he just takes her, then and there. That's why he's so bold. He must set his scene up first and then go out looking for someone. He doesn't want to miss his chance, so he doesn't wait for safety. He's not stalking them or planning where and when to take them – this is why we couldn't figure out if it was opportunistic or if there was a link between the victims. It's both."

"The last one is the jacket," Nate said, still reading. "'It was late at night when I saw them both, Leaving that bar with his jacket on her.' He saw Tessa Patinson walking out of a bar late at night wearing a man's jacket and he decided she was next."

"That's all the descriptions," Laura said. "The rest – it's about the couple being in love, not describing the woman who stole the man. Does that mean he's done?"

Nate raised his eyebrows. "Would make our jobs a hell of a lot easier if he is."

"A bit less time-sensitive, maybe," Laura said. "I don't know about easier. And we can't exactly start acting like he's done just in case he isn't. He might be about to move onto another song."

"Well, the singer only had the one song," Nate said.

"Right, but she had no emotional connection to it, remember?" Laura said. It was her turn to raise her eyebrows at him. "But you know who would have?"

"The songwriter?" Nate replied, and Laura had never been happier to find the two of them singing the same tune.

"So, let's find out who that was and what else they wrote – and who might want to get revenge on their behalf today," Laura said, feeling at last like they had a shot of bringing this killer down.

CHAPTER TWENTY ONE

There was a certain amount of ritual involved in setting up a new spot. It wasn't intentional, really, but it had happened on the first one and since then he'd found himself repeating the same steps. Like it was luck. If he managed to get away with it the first time, then he had to carry on doing the same thing to avoid being caught every time after that.

And it was imperative he didn't get caught. After all, he had to save his work. He had to do this for his grandmother. It was his responsibility now, and if he let her down, he was never going to forgive himself.

It started with the case. The sun was dipping below the horizon as he climbed the stairs to the attic, where he carefully removed the case from one of the storage boxes stacked up at the side of the room. Then, he walked up to the gramophone he had chosen earlier and sat in front of it, contemplating it for a moment. He picked it up carefully and packed it into the case where it would be safe, making sure that it was done slowly and with love so that the antique device would not be damaged or jostled. The last step was to find the record, taking it out of the display case he'd set up with all of them, and to place it inside with the gramophone.

The rope, the method he had chosen for ending them, and the bottle with the rag went into his own bag – nowhere near the delicate and important parts of this. He was too late into the game now to risk damaging something and having the record not be able to play.

All he had to do was this one, and it would be over.

He closed his eyes with the lightest smile, stroking a hand over the closed and zipped case. Just one more horrible thing he had to do, and it would be over. All of the problems they'd been having were going to go away. His grandmother would be healthy again. She could be discharged from the hospital. And she wouldn't be mad at him anymore. She'd be grateful.

Or maybe she wouldn't even notice, or realize it was his efforts that saved her. That was fine, too. All he wanted was that she could come home. One more thing to do, and then she would be home and everything would be fine. Everything would be right back to normal. Even better than normal, actually.

When she was back, things would be wonderful.

He just had to make sure that he got this one thing done, for her.

He checked the case one more time, ticking off all of the elements one by one to be sure he had them. Then he ran through the scenario in his head, trying to make sure he had covered all eventualities and there was nothing that had slipped his mind.

He would go to the place he knew he needed to go – that was not something he needed to pack, but rather something he carried with him already: the information in his head. Then he would find the person who needed to be there – he would know them when the time came.

Next, he would use the bottle and the rag (check) to make sure they couldn't fight back. Then the ropes to make sure they couldn't escape (check). Next he'd set up the gramophone (check) and the record (check) – he would have to be quick about it, which was going to be strange because for the other three he'd been able to prepare ahead of time. He had to make sure his hands didn't shake, that he didn't drop or damage anything.

Then they would dance. Finally, he would end them with the largest item he was going to carry – check. Afterwards, he'd need to call the police – but he already knew where he could find a public phone nearby, and that wasn't going to take long at all.

It seemed he had everything he needed.

He was ready.

He took a deep breath and lifted both the bag and the case, holding them, testing their weight.

He was ready.

He nodded to himself one last time and started to climb down out of the attic, eyes ahead, aiming for the front door and the waiting night.

CHAPTER TWENTY TWO

Laura placed the printout down right in the middle of all their other notes, crime scene photographs, and research.

"Earl Maverford," she said, triumphantly.

Nate peered at the piece of paper. "This is him?"

"Yep," Laura said. Finding a photograph of him hadn't been easy. She would have given up, if she hadn't randomly stumbled across one while looking up his discography. It looked like it had been taken at a family gathering, not used for a record or the press. Maverford was wearing a suit, smiling, dark hair and dark eyes becoming almost obscured in the low-quality reproduction photograph. "There's a lot more to it, too. I managed to find a blog post going into his work which talks about the song."

"Why didn't we see this before?" Nate asked in some surprise.

"Because it was way down on the tenth page even of the search for his name," Laura replied. "Let alone any other search. But this post has a lot of information which I think we'd never be able to hear any better even if we got it from the horse's mouth. There was a lot going on behind the scenes at this record label."

"Go on," Nate said.

"It wasn't just the singer who was desperate to make it big," Laura said. "The songwriter was the same. They were all part of the same studio, owned by the record label. It was a kind of development farm before that was a concept. They were all vying for a chance to really work with the record label, but as the blog post puts it, they only had one shot to make it."

"If they didn't sell big, the label dropped them completely?" Nate asked.

Laura nodded. "So, the songwriter – Maverford – wrote this song thinking that he would pitch it for one of the big voices of the day. Maybe Ella Fitzgerald or Billie Holiday."

Nate gave a low whistle. "Billie would have made it a hit, for sure."

"Well, that's what he thought. But the record label had other ideas. They decided they wanted to give it to a singer from the same stable – a nobody. Nena Flora. They were trying to launch her career and they decided to give her this song to do it, only she flopped, like Jack told us."

"But didn't the writer just write more songs?" Nate asked.

"He did, but he never managed to get one of those bigger singers to sing his music," Laura said. "He felt like his career was ruined because his one big song, the best he'd ever written, ended up in the hands of this nobody and she didn't do it justice. Later in life he did interviews where he claimed that he was stifled after that, never given a big chance. And the only reason we really know about all this was that he outlived many of his contemporaries. He spoke about it right towards the end of his life when the rest of them had passed on and he was the only one left to give insight about what it was like back then."

"Just like Nena, he went to the grave believing his career was ruined," Nate said. "This one song has a lot to answer for."

"And just like with Nena, I wonder if that chip on his shoulder wasn't passed down through his descendants," Laura said.

Nate sat up in front of the computer, doing a search on the name Maverford. "There's a Mark Maverford living locally. He has a parking fine on record. No fingerprints."

"That could be promising," Laura said. "Anything on date of birth or address?"

"I've got both," Nate said, reading from the screen. "He's twenty-five and lives downtown."

"Then we need to go downtown," Laura said. "Because if we though that Jack Flora was a good suspect, then surely Mark Maverford has to be an even stronger one."

"I'll drive," Nate grinned, swiping his keys from the desk. It felt like they were finally getting somewhere, after all the false turns – and Laura could feel the killer almost within their grasp.

**

Laura looked up at the apartment building, squinting in the gloom. There were streetlights outside, but they didn't go up as far as the floor that Mark Maverford was listed as living on.

"I hope to God they have an elevator," she said, and Nate snorted.

"I'll race you up there," he said.

"I hope you're joking," Laura said. "Because you know I'm competitive enough that I would take you up on it, and by the time we got to the top, neither of us would be in any fit state to arrest a suspect."

"I'm joking," Nate smiled. "Come on. Let's go find the elevator."

They moved inside the building after a group of teenagers who had unlocked the lobby door with a key, managing to get inside without alerting anyone they were there. Seeing an elevator right there in the lobby, Laura breathed a sigh of relief and hit the call button.

The lobby was dirty, the carpets stained and leaflets half-falling off a communal noticeboard. There was graffiti across some of the mailboxes. Nate followed her glances and lifted his chin. "Looks like Mark Maverford didn't inherit the kind of legacy a music legend would want to leave behind."

"No, he didn't," Laura agreed. "And he's not even doing as well as Jack Flora, judging by this – which is saying something."

The elevator pinged an announcement of its arrival and the doors swished open, prompting Laura and Nate to step inside. It smelled like stale cigarette smoke, and Laura found herself holding her breath as they waited for it to take them all the way up to the fifteenth floor.

"At least he can't run out the back door in a place like this," Nate muttered. He was clearly gritting his teeth against the smell as well.

"I don't know," she said, teasing him. She remembered another case they'd worked where the suspect had been a bit more inventive. "If there's a balcony, he might try to jump down into a pool or something else that will break his fall."

"Thankfully, I don't think this place has a pool," Nate replied drily.

The doors pinged and whooshed open, and Laura stepped out gratefully – though the hall wasn't much better. It was bare concrete up here, an open view down to the courtyard below where they had entered the building. In the darkness, she felt even more exposed than she might normally – though she reminded herself that it had been hard to see up here from the ground past the glow of the streetlights.

Laura stopped short, finding herself in front of the door they wanted quicker than expected, and put out a hand to stop Nate walking into her.

"Right," he said, squaring his shoulders, and then nodded to her.

Laura knocked loud and hard on the door.

There was a sound of movement inside, like someone had jumped, startled by the knock. Then more movement, what sounded like muttering, and finally the door clicked open.

"Who are you?" the man who answered the door said. He was holding the door half-closed with the chain in place, peering out in the gap below it. Laura assessed his face. He looked about the right age, and she thought she could see a trace of resemblance to the photograph of Earl Maverford she had seen.

"Mark Maverford?" Laura asked. She saw Nate subtly shift his posture, putting his toe close to the door, ready to block it from shutting.

"Who wants to know?" he asked, his eyes shifting between them rapidly. Something wasn't right here. Something in his manner was off. Laura found herself bracing, her hand going towards her hip but pausing short of touching her gun.

"Mr. Maverford, we'd like to discuss something with you about your great-grandfather," Laura said. "Earl Maverford. Do you know much about him?" She didn't want to use the word 'FBI' until she had to, not until the chain was off the door. Right now, he could easily slam it in their faces.

"Oh, you here about great-grandpop?" he said, becoming more animated. "Did you know him?"

Laura shot a sideways glance at Nate. Surely neither of them looked like they could be that old. "No, we didn't," she said. "That's why we'd like to ask you about him."

"Dope," Maverford said. There was a rattle as the chain came off the door. "Well, come the hell in, friends!"

He stepped back and walked into the apartment, away from the door, leaving them standing there. He was dancing a little as he walked, even though there was no music playing. An abrupt shift from suspicion to what looked like euphoria – Laura wasn't sure, but…

There was a potential that either drugs or mental health issues were at play here, and either way, she didn't want to spook this suspect.

She gestured to Nate who nodded approval, and they both stepped inside. Nate closed the door behind them as Laura found her way to an open kitchen – dining – living space, where Maverford had already thrown himself casually across a beaten-up old sofa covered with a giant howling wolf blanket.

The place was a mess. The coffee table was littered with empty cigarette cartons, empty beer bottles and cans, and other detritus. Laura spotted at least a couple of scraps of foil and empty plastic bags amongst them. Those could be clear signs of drug use. They had to be careful here.

The lights were dim, but still – looking closely at Maverford, she couldn't help but think his pupils were unusually sized.

"How much do you know about Earl Maverford and his music?" Nate asked. The question was cautious, as if he was trying to get Maverford to say something about the song without being prompted, and Laura decided to follow his lead.

"I know a lot about him," he said, pointing to a beaten-up chair with a sunken cushion. "Take a seat, go on, be at home. Ask me anything you want to know. You want a puff?"

He pulled out what looked like a rolled joint from a pocket and, before either Laura or Nate could react, lit it.

"Is that for medical use?" Nate asked uneasily. Laura echoed the sentiment. They didn't want to get bogged down in a petty drug charge before they even got anywhere. Then again, if they had something to arrest him over, it would make getting him to the station a lot easier.

And then again, if he was high, they wouldn't have a great time questioning him – and most lawyers would be able to get his testimony thrown out unless he said something only the killer could possibly know.

"What are you, feds or something?" Maverford asked, in a casual tone, like he was making a joke.

Wordlessly, Nate drew his badge out and opened it up, showing him that they were, in fact, feds.

Maverford swore and scrambled to his feet, dropping the joint and stomping on it – though more because he was moving in an agitated manner than out of any concern for burning the place down, Laura thought.

"You can't do that!" he yelled. "You've got to tell me if you're police or whatever! You're not allowed to just come in here and – that's entrapment – that's illegal!"

"I didn't actually say anything or ask you for the drugs," Nate pointed out. Laura was beginning to get the impression, too, that it might have been more than just cannabis in the home-rolled joint. "You offered it to us. But I'd like to talk to you about something totally different – about Earl Maverford. I think it's a good idea if you come to the local precinct with us to answer a few questions, and maybe sober up."

Laura winced internally. She didn't have a feeling that Mark was going to accept this so easily.

"No way," he said, quickly stepping back and almost tripping over onto his own sofa. "No way, man. You can't take me in. I won't go. I'm not going."

"Look, right now this is a request," Nate said. Laura started to move towards the door, thinking about blocking exits. "If you want, we can make it official and arrest you. Is that what you want?"

"You can't arrest me!" Maverford shouted. "I haven't done anything!"

Nate sighed and glanced at Laura. She nodded.

"Mark Maverford," he said. "I'm arresting you on suspicion of possession of illegal drugs." He stepped closer towards Mark, taking a pair of handcuffs out and reaching out for the man's hands, but Mark only freaked out even more. He put his hands up in front of himself and lashed out wildly, swiping Nate's hands away whenever he started to get close.

"Mr. Maverford!" Laura shouted, trying to get him to calm down by listening to her voice. He only flailed harder, and at last she stepped in beside Nate to try and wrestle the man's arms down far enough to get the cuffs around both of his wrists at once. The whole time he yelled incoherent complaints into their ears about how they couldn't arrest him for entrapment over medicinal drugs, until finally Laura and Nate between them managed to get him cuffed and under control.

"Right," Laura said, blowing a bit of hair out of her face that had fallen out of her ponytail – she had no way to move it, with both her hands firmly holding Maverford in place in case he tried to run off. "Let's get him back to the precinct. I think we need to have a serious chat about what you've been doing for the past few days, Mark."

CHAPTER TWENTY THREE

"Great," Laura sighed, shaking her head. "So, we're not going to be able to question him yet?"

"I'm afraid not," the medical officer said, shaking her head. "He's still got a high enough concentration of drugs in his system that anything you would be able to get him to say would be inadmissible in court, anyway. I would recommend waiting until tomorrow to even begin interviewing him. In the meantime, he should stay under medical supervision in case of any adverse reactions."

Nate hit his hand against the side of the desk, and Laura couldn't help but agree with the sentiment. "Can we not even ask exploratory questions? Come back to him tomorrow with the full formal interview and go over the same ground?"

She shook her head. "I wouldn't advise it. There's room for an attorney to argue that his client had suggestions pushed into his memory when he was under the influence, leading to a coerced confession."

Laura sighed. What a nightmare. It wasn't like she was in any rush to get home at the moment, but it was just too frustrating to have to sit around here and wait for the suspect to be ready for them. They had him. All she wanted to do was get on with the interview, get him to confess, so this whole thing could be put to bed for good.

"It doesn't matter," Nate said, shaking his head, though he sounded frustrated too. "We have him. We know we do. He has everything in place – he's a descendent of the songwriter and has a close personal connection to the song, he doesn't appear to have any kind of alibi because he doesn't work, he's definitely psychotic…"

"I don't know," Laura said, biting her lip. "We should talk to Captain Kinnock, find out if there's been any progress with the search of the apartment."

"Fine," Nate shrugged, nodding thanks to the doctor, and then jerking his chin up towards Kinnock's office. "Looks like he's in there. Let's go ask."

Laura led the way, driven by a kind of urge to get to the bottom of this sooner rather than later. Something was nagging at her. Gnawing.

It was a feeling she got sometimes that she almost never liked. Usually because it meant she'd gone wrong somewhere, and she was going to have to start again.

She knocked only briefly before pushing the captain's door open, not waiting for him to give her permission. She didn't care. As far as she was concerned, if this case really was about to be over, it didn't matter if he liked her or not. In fact, it didn't matter in the first place. They were FBI. He had to do what he was asked, or face federal charges himself.

"Ah, agents," he said, seemingly not phased by the intrusion. "I've just had a report back from the senior detective at the suspect's home. You're going to like it."

"Oh?" Nate prompted.

"There's a copy of the record in his home, as well as a gramophone," Kinnock grinned. "Well done. It was a masterclass, honestly. I'm pleased to say that our town won't be haunted by this danger any longer. I'll be holding a press conference in a couple of hours to reassure our citizens, and you're welcome to join me."

That felt premature – and besides, Laura would do a lot of things to get out of appearing on television. Not quite anything, but a lot of things. "Just one gramophone?" she asked. Something about that jarred her. For a second she thought it was because three gramophones had been purchased and three already used, but then her mind sorted the facts into their respective sources and she remembered that the purchase had been nothing more than mistaken identity.

The captain shrugged. "Just one. I guess we stopped him before he committed his final murder. Or maybe he was planning to go out and get more once he'd used up his supply; I can't be sure."

"That's good news," Nate said, nudging Laura's shoulder with a grin. "We were right on time."

"Yeah," Laura said, though inwardly she just wasn't sure.

What was this feeling? Why was she still getting it?

As they walked back to their desks, Nate chatting casually about how he would love to go back and get some rest and then tackle the suspect tomorrow, Laura's mind was busy elsewhere. She was trying to think this feeling through. She was starting to liken it to the aura of death she got when around someone whose demise was imminent. It wasn't an aura or a vision or anything like that, not exactly – just a tightening in her gut.

Maybe it wasn't related to her visions at all. Maybe it was just that – gut instinct. But still. She couldn't help wondering if it was something stronger.

It had never let her down before.

"I'm just going to go over my notes again," Laura said, realizing only when she finished that she must have cut Nate off mid-sentence.

He looked at her hard for a moment, then glanced around. "Are you seeing something?" he asked in a low voice.

"No," Laura said. She shook her head. "Maybe it's nothing. But I just…"

"Let's go back over the notes," Nate suggested. "I should check we have everything we need for tomorrow, anyway, so we're not blindsided if he gets some fancy lawyer all of a sudden who knows how to twist things."

"Right," Laura said. They reached their desk and she saw, pulling her notebook out right away and flipping to the pages that were calling to her. The pages with the lyrics of the song she had written down.

She went over it all one more time.

She came along, with a rose in her hair
Pretty and young, with a smile like sunshine
How could I know that he'd put it there?
Or that she'd taken the man that was mine?

That had to be Dakota Henson, didn't it? There was no other way to make the lyrics fit the other girls. Dakota was the one with the flower in her hair, and she was certainly pretty and young. Laura could picture her smiling on the way to the store. That was her.

He was so fine, I thought I was lucky
A husband, a child, the future I saw
She was this maid from down in Kentucky
Red hair that reached almost down to the floor

Kentucky, though, didn't fit with Jenna Janes. And while Laura had been over it and over it, deciding that the connections he was making were visual… still. What if the killer heard someone with a Kentucky accent and decided to take them, too? But then again, if the killer was in custody, what did it matter? He couldn't hurt anyone from the medical bay.

It was late at night when I saw them both
Leaving that bar with his jacket on her
I couldn't believe it, yes I was loath
To think that coat was a gift from my sir

And that one, it had to be their last victim, Tessa Patinson. She'd come out of the party with her men's jacket on, looking like she'd just come from a date maybe. Sad as it was, that had been enough.

The lyrics fit. The perpetrator fit.

Didn't he?

The thing she kept going back to was that apartment. The way it had been so messy, littered with drug paraphernalia and old takeout packaging and all the rest of it. It was filthy. It looked like Maverford was no stranger to falling asleep on the couch and not bothering to clean up the next morning. Getting high or drunk and then repeating it again the next day.

That kind of environment... it didn't point to the organized and tightly methodical mind of their killer. That killer was calculating and had a steady hand, an ability to repeat the same pattern exactly, again and again.

Laura wasn't a forensic psychologist, but she would have expected something different from the profile. A tidy home, probably a neat and well-preserved shrine to the past. Somewhere that was frozen in time. The killer would have a place for everything, a neat order to both his life and his home. That was what she had been expecting.

Laura scanned over the song again. There was no other description of a woman in the lyrics. Just the thing about Kentucky, which she was fairly sure had nothing new to bring – the killer had taken it stanza by stanza, and that one was all about Jenna Janes. There was nothing left but the opening stanza, which was about the singer herself, and the closing two, which were only about how the man and woman grew closer.

Except...

They were on the bridge, their breath was misting
When I looked up and saw them both up there
My watch, it stopped when I saw them kissing
My man and the girl with the rose in her hair

That was different, wasn't it? At first glance, Laura had taken it differently – that it was about the girl with the rose in her hair again, and Dakota Henson was already dead, so it couldn't mean anything. But what if...

What if there was one more character left to be drawn out of the song?

The important part of this lyric was the bridge. Two people kissing on a bridge. It had to mean something. Had they really caught him before he was able to use one more gramophone on the last victim?

Or…

"Thought you might like to see this."

Laura looked up to see Captain Kinnock holding a printout in his hand. He was grinning.

"What is it?" she asked, while Nate frowned from beside her.

"The final pieces of the puzzle," Kinnock said, handing them over. "You can use these tomorrow to get him to confess, I bet. They just came through from our evidence photographer."

Laura stared at the pictures. A copy of the record – and a gramophone.

But it wasn't the same type of gramophone that had been used in the first three murders at all.

Now, she knew.

They had the wrong man.

CHAPTER TWENTY FOUR

"This isn't done," Laura said, turning to Nate urgently.

He looked from the photographs and back to her, slowly. "Are you thinking it's the wrong gramophone?"

"Of course, it's the wrong gramophone," Laura said. "What do we know about the crime scenes so far?"

"They're all exactly the same," Nate sighed, picking up on what she was getting at immediately.

"Do we have the results back on the fingerprint analysis?" Laura asked. There was still the print evidence. They could still get the answers from that.

"It wasn't a match," Captain Kinnock shrugged. "It was probably just contamination. Someone else touched the scene that we don't know about, or maybe the print was on there before the killer ever used it. It doesn't matter. We'll get enough evidence to put him away, and you'll get the confession tomorrow, so we're all good."

"No, we're not," Laura said. "This means he might not be the killer!"

"You're overthinking it," Captain Kinnock said with a careless gesture. "Loosen up. You can talk to him tomorrow and he'll probably explain he couldn't get more than three gramophones from the same place. Relax and go back to your motel, or go for a drink to celebrate. This is a great result. You got it done so quickly, I think there's room for a promotion or two all around – or even just a pay raise." He started to wander away with those words of advice, and Laura shook her head at his disappearing back.

"He just wants to look good in front of the town," she said, her voice low. "He's thinking with his pocket, not his head. Closing cases too early is probably how he got to captain so young anyway."

Nate gave her a half-smirk. "Careful," he said. "You might end up sounding jealous. Anyway, you're preaching to the choir. Something about this doesn't smell right."

"Exactly," Laura said. "And if it doesn't smell right, then I don't think it's right. There's another verse that hasn't been touched on yet. The one about the bridge."

"You think the real killer is still out there, and he's going to strike on a bridge tonight?"

"Got it in one," Laura nodded. Once again she reminisced on how much better it was to be back working with Nate – someone who understood the way she worked and could almost read her mind at times. "How many bridges do you think there could be in town here?"

Nate didn't waste a moment. "There's one way to find out," he said, spinning back to face the computer and opening up the online map.

"What constitutes a bridge, also?" Laura asked, thinking out loud.

"What do you mean?" Nate frowned. "A bridge is a bridge."

"No, there are different kinds," Laura argued. "A traditional bridge is over water, but you could also have a footbridge or a rail bridge. An overpass could maybe be a bridge. You could even have a bridge inside a shopping mall – you know, you get those pathways across the sides of the upper floor."

Nate threw his hands in the air for a moment, clearly at a loss. "Well, hell, I don't know. I didn't know we would need to be bridge experts."

"What does the map tell us?" Laura asked, leaning closer. "There's a river in town, right?"

"Right, but it only cuts through the north area, which is mostly residential," Nate said. "Look, it's hardly even within the limits."

Laura thought for a moment, one of her fingernails sneaking its way into her mouth where she could chew it. She needed to get this right. It needed to be right, or the real killer was going to get away. She was sure, now, beyond sure, that Mark Maverford was just a junkie.

And if the song was the key to all of this as she truly believed, then there was just one more victim to go. After that, the killer would disappear into the night. Maybe they would never find him, unless his prints turned up in a random check years from now.

"The killer we're looking for is into the traditional," she said. "Old gramophone, old record, old, abandoned places. We're looking for somewhere with history. I think it has to be the traditional kind of bridge, doesn't it?"

"I get where you're coming from," Nate said. He zoomed the map in on the river, scrolling across it with a close eye. "Looks like four or five bridges."

"We need more information about each of them," Laura said. "When they were built, what they look like."

"Alright, hold on, hold on," Nate said, navigating to a new tab so he could try a new search. He found a page about the bridges of the town, part of a historical society website, and opened it up. "Let's see…"

Laura read over his shoulder, too impatient to wait. "The newest ones were built in the seventies, so they're out. And look, this one was from the sixties. It's old, but I don't feel like it's old enough."

"Then it's one of the last two," Nate said, scrolling further down. "Here we are. They both date back to the early 1900s. They've been rebuilt and refurbished a few times, but at least there was always a bridge there. It sounds like the others were only built as the town expanded enough to take in more of the river."

"I don't feel like this killer would do all of this and then just go to some modern bridge," Laura said. "Think about it. It's all old-fashioned. I really think he'll choose one of those two."

"But which one?" Nate asked.

Laura bit her lip. The site had low-quality images of all the bridges, and the two older models looked almost identical. They were around the same age, around the same design… what would make them stand out for the killer?

"I don't know," she admitted. "There's no further detail in the verse. Just that the singer is looking up and sees them kissing. Someone could do that on either of those bridges."

"Right," Nate said, rubbing his forehead. "Well, I don't like it, but this is a good lead and we can't ignore it. I think we have to split up."

"I agree," Laura said, relieved. For a moment she thought he was going to say he didn't like the idea and they should forget about it. "I'll go to the one to the west, you go to the one to the east. Deal?"

"Deal," Nate said, turning off the monitor and shooting out of his chair like they were in a race.

Maybe, if the killer was out there stalking his next victim, they were.

***

Nate pulled up the borrowed car by the bridge, finding a quieter road to leave it on where he was in sight of the structure and close enough to rush over there fast. Getting out of the car, he found himself emerging into a cool and quiet night. There was almost no noise except for the low hum of traffic elsewhere in town and the quiet lapping of water against the sides of the riverbank. He started to walk to the bridge, leaning over slightly as his steps brought him closer to the bank. The water was dark, reflecting the streetlights in dappled patterns.

Nate straightened up and focused his sights on the bridge. It was lit, too – a single tall light right in the center that cast a beam across the middle part but left the two entrances dark. If he stayed near the foot of the bridge, he might be completely invisible to anyone who was on it.

He paused in the spot he deemed to be the most appropriate, looking down to check his watch. The face lit up as he tilted it; he'd made it here in good time. Better than Laura, most likely, who was going to the further bridge. Even with having to flag down a passing detective and request their vehicle, he'd arrived here pretty fast.

He settled in to wait, his eyes roving up and down the bridge for any sign of movement. It was a chilly night but not an unpleasant one. The cold struck at his exposed face, but with his hands in the pockets of his FBI windbreaker it wasn't so bad. He took up an easy pose, one that didn't stress his body too much, and found himself slipping into the quiet mentality he employed on stakeouts. He could stand here for hours – though he hoped he wasn't going to have to.

Nate's senses were all on high alert as his body drifted off, ignoring one to focus on the other. His eyes constantly scanned the bridge and his ears filtered out the sounds of the river and the traffic, searching for any anomaly. A small splash to his left made him look around, but he soon guessed it must have been a fish or something moving under the water.

He settled down again, waiting.

He felt tight like a string on a bow, waiting to be played. Taut. Every muscle in his body was ready to spring, despite his relaxed stance. One hint, and he'd be up there, grabbing whoever he needed to grab to stop someone else from dying.

There was a small movement far away, at the other side of the bridge in the gloom. Nate narrowed his eyes, trying to make it out. What was that? A person?

Yes, it was a person. He could see them more and more clearly as they came across the bridge. No – it wasn't one person, but two. A couple. They were holding hands.

Nate's breath caught in his throat. How did the song go? *Their fingers entwined while mine, they were numb.* A couple walking along a bridge holding hands – it was almost perfect. All they had to do now was…

The couple paused under the light, looking down at the water. After a moment, they turned to one another. It was cold enough that their breath misted around them as they spoke, making brief halos around their heads that caught the light perfectly.

They leaned towards one another and kissed, and then the man nuzzled his partner for one more second before turning to walk away.

"See you tomorrow," he called over his shoulder, loud enough for Nate to hear in the stillness of the night.

The woman called something back not quite as loud and then lingered there on the bridge, watching him. After a moment she turned to look down at the water again, seemingly lost in her own thoughts.

She turned to go at last, and Nate swept his eyes up and down the length of the bridge, watching for movement. His heart was thudding hard in his chest. If anyone was going to strike, the time would be now. She had fulfilled all the criteria of the song.

Nate caught something right at the far end of the bridge. Someone moving fast.

Running. Someone running.

This was it.

He grabbed his gun from its holster and sprang forwards, rushing right past the now-alarmed woman and planting his feet on the bridge before the runner caught up to them. "Freeze right there!" he yelled. "FBI! Hands above your head!"

The runner stuttered, his motion causing him to almost stumble before he came to a juddering halt. He raised his hands in the air with a jerky movement. The light above them cast a garish look down onto his features. Nate could see that his eyes were wide, shocked.

"Get down on the ground!" Nate shouted, but even he could see that something wasn't right here. Something didn't fit.

"I – I was just out for a run," the man said, his voice sounding timorous. Scared. He was getting down on the ground, starting to kneel one leg at a time, his hands still in the air. "I haven't done anything, haven't done anything at all."

Nate looked him over, approaching closer. The man lay out flat, his hands still reaching above his head, touching the surface of the bridge. With a swift movement, Nate took one hand off his gun and frisked the guy's pockets.

A cell phone and a wallet.

No rope, no sedatives, no cloth to hold against anyone's face.

This wasn't the killer.

Nate stepped back, holstering his gun. "Alright, you're clear," he said. "I apologize for the inconvenience, sir. You can go on your way."

The runner scrambled to his feet, still wide-eyed. He looked like he wanted to ask what was going on, but instead he just started running again, no doubt in fear of being shot if he lingered.

Nate raised his hands to his head, buffing them over the top of his short hair, looking around in all directions. He spun in a circle. There was no one else here. Of course, that didn't mean that the killer wasn't here, that he hadn't retreated when he saw Nate come out, but…

It had been the perfect set-up. A man and a woman kissing on the bridge, exactly like in the song. And no one had emerged from the shadows to go after them.

The killer wasn't here.

Which meant that in all likelihood, he was at Laura's bridge.

Nate turned and rushed back towards his car, knowing he needed to get to her as soon as possible.

CHAPTER TWENTY FIVE

He parked carefully, far enough from the bridge that he wouldn't raise suspicion but close enough that he would be able to get the next one back to the car. He had to make sure he wasn't caught. He knew the police were looking for him, of course – he wasn't stupid. But he had to make this final one work.

His grandmother was depending on him.

He got out of the car, tracing the lyrics of the song like an old favorite mantra in his head. *They were on the bridge, their breath was misting/When I looked up and saw them both up there.* As soon as he thought about it for even a second, he'd known where he needed to go. It had to be here.

The oldest bridge in town. A bridge that had been here when Nena Flora recorded the song. An authentic place. Grandmother would have appreciated the symbolism so much. She would have called it romantic. She still could, when he told her about all of this later. When she was better again.

He walked to the foot of the bridge and then under it slightly, on the banks of the river, where he could look up. He needed to look up and see them. That was how it would work. He had to see them from below, like the song said.

He settled in, ready to wait. To wait all night if he needed to. And if nothing came along, he'd wait tomorrow night as well – though he had a feeling that someone would come. They always did. It was like the universe wanted him to complete his mission, too.

It would all end with this one. It was a strange thought. He'd been preparing for this for so long. He'd started to collect the records when he noticed his grandmother was getting sick, long before she agreed to go to the hospital. When she started to lose things. When she said the same thing to him three times in the same day because she kept forgetting.

At first, he hadn't known why. He was just collecting them because he loved her and because she loved the song. Loved it so much it had become a soundtrack to all of his memories of her. She played it again and again, and when he knew that she was starting to fade he bought more and more of them with the cash he had saved in a piggy bank since he first moved in with her, as if that would help.

It had only been recently that he'd been shown the way – realized exactly what he could do to help, and how the records would play into it.

The song played in his mind perfectly, note for note and word for word. He didn't need to set it on one of the gramophones his grandmother had spent her life collecting in order to hear it. It was so much a part of his very being that he could play the whole thing in his head without pause, knowing he hadn't missed so much as a beat.

A few people walked over the bridge, but he ignored them. They didn't fit. It wasn't them he was looking for. He would know when he saw the one he needed.

Sitting there gave him time to think. To remember. And wasn't that the most fitting thing, to sit and think about her while he prepared to make the final connection that would save her? He remembered dancing to the song together, how she would snap without provocation – so much more lately than she ever had. He could replay the slaps like a montage of himself growing from a boy to a man, and all set to the soundtrack of that song.

How could he have heard it so many times, and yet taken so long to notice the actual meaning behind the words?

He had almost missed the connection, almost missed the roadmap that was saving his grandmother from the demons that were plaguing her. How many years had they spent, both of them, suffering for no reason?

At least he was making up for it now.

His memory touched on the day he'd first heard the song, the day he'd gone to stay with his grandmother, and he jerked away from that thought like he had touched a burning coal. It was too raw still, even after a decade. The day he'd been taken from his own home, his bedroom, and told that his parents were gone. Grandmother had been his only solace. His protector. The black dresses she wore those months had soaked up all of his tears, until he'd been able to dance with her to the song and even smile, and one day even laugh.

She had saved him from that awful emptiness. Now he was repaying the favor.

Another person stepped onto the bridge and he lifted his head, but dropped it again. A dog walker. Not his target. He couldn't just take anyone. That wouldn't do. This one, most of all, needed to be special.

He wasn't even sure who he was waiting for, but he knew that he would understand when he saw them.

He had everything set up and waiting. The warehouse was ready. The gramophone and the record were set up there, lovingly paired together, standing polished and ready for their final song. It was going to be a good one. They all were, but this one, being the last, would be the most magical. This was where it was all going to happen.

He sat idly dreaming, one hand cupping his chin so he could lean and rest, conserving his energy. The bottle in his pocket clinked when he shifted, and he rearranged the cloth around it to keep it secure.

He just had to wait, and then all of this would come together, and he would get the grandmother he knew he deserved. The one who loved and danced with him, the one who held his hands in the kitchen and lifted him up high when he was a boy, the one who showed him how to bake a cake. Not the other one, the one who snapped and snarled and hit and slapped. That demon would be gone forever.

Someone moved onto the bridge, and he sat straight, his eyes piercing the night to make her out.

A woman, alone. No man. He had always thought the last one would be a man. But he saw her there, and he knew that the universe was telling him to change his plan. It was this or wait until tomorrow because there was no way he could take anyone else now that he had seen her.

He stood up and moved silently, stealthily, across the bank of the river towards the foot of the bridge.

Tonight, she would be his, and the circle would be complete.

He took the bottle out of his pocket and tipped it upside down against the rag, making sure it was fully soaked, and crept out onto the bridge with his eyes on her back. And if there was any doubt that she was to be the one, when he heard what she was saying on the phone to her lover, all of his doubt disappeared.

CHAPTER TWENTY SIX

Nate peered ahead as he pulled up towards the bridge, narrowing his eyes to try to see better in the darkness. Where was she…?

He was uncomfortably aware that if he walked out into the light and spooked the killer, he was going to jeopardize the whole operation. The guy might end up walking free – or worse, going off and killing someone somewhere else. He couldn't risk that. If Laura was smart, she would have found a place somewhere off to the side, in the shadows. Somewhere you could watch but not be seen.

Nate parked off to the side off the road and then took his cell phone out of his pocket, dialing Laura's number. If she had her phone on her… She wasn't enough of a rookie to have the ringer set to loud. It would be on vibrate, and she'd hear it buzzing in her pocket. That way, he could ask her where she was and join her quietly.

The line rang, rang, rang.

It went to voicemail before she picked up, and Nate chewed his lip. He was starting to get a sinking feeling.

What if the reason he couldn't see Laura was that she simply wasn't there?

Nate got out of the car and turned in a circle, trying to think. He couldn't see anyone at all. There was the mission – trying to catch their killer – and then there was the basic rule of making sure that your partner was safe. It wasn't right to let her get herself into danger.

He thought about the burn on her hand – the one she'd sustained in the case he wasn't able to work with her. The one where she'd rushed in and got herself caught by the killer. Almost became his last victim. Laura was like that. She would rush in and not ask for help, only thinking about the primary mission and forgetting to keep herself safe.

It was Nate's job to do that for her. That was something he'd come to understand lately. Since she'd come clean about her powers, he'd had some doubts about his own performance. About whether he was really necessary as part of their team, or was just there to hold her hand. But he saw it now.

The reason she needed someone with her was to stop her going off the deep end. But she wasn't here. She wasn't at the bridge.

Nate threw caution to the wind and started to walk, quick march, across the bridge. He was all too aware of the sound of his boots on the wood, of the fact that he must have stuck out like a sore thumb under the bright light right in the center. He knew that anyone who had been anywhere near the last crime scene might have witnessed him attending and seen what he looked like. If the killer was here, he would be long gone before Nate ever got to the other side of the bridge. He was risking the whole stakeout.

But he believed in Laura, believed in her skills as a cop as well as her powers, and he knew she had to be right about the bridge. And that meant if she wasn't here…

Nate reached the other side and swore under his breath. He gave himself a minute to adjust to the darkness again, walking a little way in either direction to the sides of the bridge. He didn't see anything. No one whispered his name in the darkness to call him out of sight.

He hesitated in the softer mud by the bank of the river, looking down. A pair of footprints in the mud. Boots. Women's size. The kind of boots that were standard wear for FBI agents.

Laura had been standing here, and she wasn't here anymore.

Nate swore again, louder, and grabbed his phone out of his pocket. Still nothing from Laura. There was only one way this played out. Wherever she was, whether she had been taken by force or gone willingly to follow him – she was with the killer. And she was in a situation where she couldn't answer her phone.

She was in trouble.

"Yeah?" a voice crackled over the other end of the line.

Nate glanced around, walking quickly back to his car. "Is that Dean Marsters?"

"Speaking," Dean said. He was one of the techs at the FBI, a friend of Laura's. Nate had never really liked him for some reason, but now he needed his help.

"It's Special Agent Nate Lavoie," Nate said. "I'm in need of a trace on a phone."

"Whose phone, and do you have a warrant?" Dean asked. He sounded lazy, like he was typing with both hands and holding the phone between his ear and shoulder, not really paying attention.

"I don't need one. Special Agent Laura Frost's personal cell."

"Frost?" Now Nate could picture him sitting up and paying attention. Typical.

"Yes. I think she's in danger," Nate said urgently. "We're on a live case and she's disappeared. I need that trace as fast as you can get it." He opened the car door and hopped back inside, feeling how the warmth of the interior hit him like a slap compared to the cold out there.

"I'll call you back immediately when we have a result," Dean said, then ended the call on his end.

Nate threw the phone down on the passenger seat, gritting his teeth in a grim grimace. Nice of the guy to only take him seriously once he knew Laura was involved. But if it was going to help keep her safe, then he wasn't going to waste time chewing him out.

He also wasn't going to waste time sitting here in this nice warm car, rubbing his hands together to get the cold out, and having a jolly old time while he waited. The trace could take a while, and Laura was on her own. Nate wasn't going to leave her in danger and do nothing.

He put the car into drive and started to move, first heading over the other side of the river and then scanning the map on his cell. There were a few abandoned buildings that he could see. Lining them up with the data they'd already gathered in the course of the investigation gave him a few more. There were warehouses up ahead, but also abandoned homes and at least one store that was temporarily closed. Not abandoned, but not yet opened up again, either. Any one of them could be a good candidate for a spot to take a victim, as far as this killer was concerned.

It didn't matter how many there were. Nate had to find her.

He set his car in the direction of the nearest one and floored the gas pedal, knowing that every second he took to find her could be the second that ended her life.

CHAPTER TWENTY SEVEN

Laura had grown tired of waiting. She was beginning to think nothing was going to happen at all.

She stretched her arms above her head restlessly, tapping both of her feet on the ground, turning her ankles to ease out the kinks of standing still for so long in cold weather. She'd seen so many people cross the bridge already. It was popular even at this time of night. People tended to come in ones and twos with gaps between them, couples or strangers. She'd seen a pair – a woman and a man walking close together and talking – already, but nothing had happened.

Was the killer even here?

She thought about phoning Nate to see if he'd seen anything yet, but then thought better of it. If his cell was on ring, it might disturb the peace of the night and alert the killer that there was someone watching. She might even end up putting him in danger. She didn't want to do that just because she was feeling impatient. She waited.

But it was cold, and being near the river didn't help. She found herself rocking on the spot, shifting rapidly from foot to foot, doing anything she could to try to will some extra heat into her body. It was no use. She should have brought a longer coat, or something to keep her legs warm.

Restless, cold, tired, impatient. There was only one thing for it. Laura started to move, taking a slow stroll onto the bridge.

From here, she told herself, she just might be able to spot a suspect somewhere hiding in the darkness.

As soon as she stepped under the light that illuminated most of the bridge, she knew that had been a mistake. It was so bright up here that she could hardly see a thing. The darkness she had been comfortably standing in a moment before, at the end of the bridge, was now pitch black from her current vantage point. She couldn't make out a thing.

She turned in a circle but couldn't see anyone. It was so quiet here, in the residential part of town. Now over the center of the bridge, all she could hear was the rush of the water. There was nothing else to disturb the peace.

This was a wild goose chase. She'd been wrong, hadn't she?

She turned back to look across the other side of the bridge, wondering if she should walk over and check things out over there. There was something in the darkness, a kind of flicker, something that she thought she might or might not have imagined. She squinted, trying to see closer...

Her phone rang in her pocket, making her jump, and she almost laughed at herself. She grabbed it and saw Nate's name on the caller display, answering the call right away. She turned back to the other side of the bridge, the one she had come from, and began a slow walk back to the car.

"Hi," she said. "It's quiet here. Anything with you?"

"Laura," Nate said urgently. "He isn't here. I think he must be with you."

"No," Laura sighed. "No, Nate, I think I was wrong. I'm in the wrong place. We shouldn't even be doing this."

"No, really," Nate said. "I think you're right. Look, just because my bridge was a bust doesn't mean yours is. I really think you're right about everything. Just stay there and stay out of sight. I'm on my way to you now."

"Alright," she said. "I'll wait for you here."

"I'll be about fifteen minutes," Nate said, and then all hell broke loose.

The only thing Laura knew was that someone was on her, someone who came from behind, and they had shoved something over her nose and mouth. She tried to breathe, her hands instinctively going back to push and shove at whoever it was, trying to aim a kick at them without being able to see. Her head was pulled back, her eyes looking up at the black sky, and she found herself flailing wildly, missing her mark completely. She tried again, her arms feeling heavy, her head foggy, her eyes closing – she fought to keep them open one more time, her last impression the white light right overhead, fading into a mist that enveloped all of her senses until there was nothing left.

***

Laura opened her eyes slowly, immediately wanting to close them again as the light shot pain through her nerves. She felt sick. Like she had the most epic hangover of all time, from the kind of drinking where you were still kind of drunk when you woke up the next morning.

But she hadn't had a drink. She hadn't had a drink in a very long time. She was in AA. These facts filtered through to her slowly. She was lying on the floor. She should get up. The floor was cold. Where was the floor?

She opened her eyes properly this time, managing to blearily squint around the room. The light was gone, thankfully. The room was dim now. She was in some kind of large space, one she didn't recognize. Where was she?

It came back to her in pieces: bridge. Nate. Killer. Song.

She had been standing on the bridge talking to Nate. She remembered talking on the phone. Looking for the killer but not seeing him.

He must have seen her.

She moved her head to look up, towards another part of the room, and saw the gramophone.

He had her.

Laura's mind struggled to work through the fog that seemed to hold her in place, slowing down her thoughts and making her so heavy and tired. After-effects of the drug he had used to knock her out – that information floated through her brain like a cloud, clearing out whatever else she had been trying to think. No, she had to concentrate. She had to focus.

She'd been taken by the killer. That meant she wasn't far away from death, herself, if she couldn't get out of this. She moved her hands and feet experimentally and found them both bound tightly by ropes. Running was not an option, and neither was fighting back. That didn't mean she couldn't find a way to buy time or even get away, though.

Nate was on his way to her – but, no, he was on his way to the bridge. Not to wherever they were now. She was on her own. If she wanted to survive this, she was going to have to figure a way out herself. If she didn't think of something, and soon, through this fog that seemed to be filling her head, then she was going to die. He was going to stab her through her heart and it would be over within seconds, with no hope of even waiting for an ambulance to arrive.

If she didn't figure this out, she was dead.

She had one advantage that none of the other victims had had, at least.

She knew what was coming next.

There was a sound nearby and then she heard it: the song, playing just like it had with all the other women. Laura looked up again, craning her head, and saw him. He had his back to her, bending over the gramophone. He seemed to be enjoying the music for a moment, savoring it.

He straightened up, took what seemed to be a deep breath, and then turned towards her.

And Laura wanted to kick herself so hard, because she could have stopped all of this long ago.

"Hello, agent," Artur Oreyo said, taking care to smooth down his hair on one side as though he thought it might be out of place. The antique music store owner was dressed formally, in a black suit with a long black jacket. With his dark hair and pale skin, it made him look like an undertaker. He sketched a bow as he stood over her, then held out a hand. "Will you give me this dance?"

"Dance?" Laura looked up at him, hardly comprehending. She couldn't believe she'd missed it. The mistake he'd made mixing up phonographs and gramophones – it hadn't been a mistake at all. He'd been distracting them. Sending them on a wild goose chase to keep them busy. And they'd fallen for it. "My legs are bound. My hands, too."

"Don't worry about that," he said, almost pleasantly. He'd been so sketchy when they met him in the store. She'd thought it had been about tax evasion, or maybe illegal smuggling of prohibited materials, the kind of thing you found in antique places. But it hadn't been that at all. He was their killer. He'd been standing right in front of her, and she had ignored him and gone off in the direction he sent her. She'd wasted time, and another victim had died. "I'll support you. Here."

He reached down and did something behind her back, and Laura felt a release of tension. Her arms were free. But she wasn't stupid enough to think that they were free completely: she remembered the other victims. Bound just so they could bring their arms to their sides, and no further. She tested the ropes before bringing her hands around in front of her. They were tight still, the bindings just out of the reach of her fingers at the longest stretch.

"What about my feet?" Laura asked, chancing it just in case.

"You'll be fine," Oreyo said. There was a kind of dreamlike quality to his voice, almost as if he wasn't sure this was all real. Or like, Laura realized, he was acting out a scene. Whatever fantasy or ritual this was, he was lost in it.

"I don't fit your pattern, Artur," Laura said, trying to appeal to that, trying to break him out of the dream somehow. "I'm not one of your girls from the song."

"I didn't think you would be, either," he said. "But I saw you there talking to your lover on the bridge. That was when I knew. You'd been sent to me. Sent to finish it all. How could it be more perfect? To complete the circle with the one person who might have been able to stop me?"

There was one more person. There was Nate. And beyond him, even, there was the police force – though Captain Kinnock had come to them for help and didn't believe that Maverford was the wrong man, Laura knew that every single person on his force couldn't be incompetent. But she didn't point any of that out. Better for him to think she was the only one. Better for him to let down his guard.

"You heard wrong," Laura said. "I wasn't talking to a lover."

"You can't talk your way out of it now," he frowned. "I'm not listening to you. I heard what I heard, and I know you're the last one. I won't let you stop me from saving her."

"Saving who?" Laura asked.

"My grand- stop that," he said, frowning at her. "Stop it. Stop trying to talk your way out of this. We have to dance. That's how this starts."

"It doesn't have to," Laura said. Her tongue tasted strange inside her own mouth. She felt like she was trying to talk with half a mouthful of dry cotton. She wiggled her fingers behind her back, turning her wrists in clockwise movements, repeating the gesture over and over to try to get some purchase.

Artur made a gesture of annoyance, twisting his face at her. "You're doing it again," he said. "And we're wasting time. Now, listen. We're going to have to start the song again."

As he walked away, Laura listened to the refrain playing out. *Oh, my man and the rose, Oh, how the story goes…*

All she needed to do was keep him distracted, keep him talking, stop him from doing what he said he needed to do. If she managed that, made him keep going back to start the record again, she could keep buying herself time. One minute, two minutes, here and there.

With his back turned to her, Laura started reaching, trying to see if she could bend her body far enough to touch the ropes around her ankles.

There was a sudden abrupt silence. Oreyo set the gramophone up again, ready to play from the beginning. There was a pregnant pause and then the song began again, slowly filtering up through the air, lending far more of a languorous mood to the occasion than Laura actually felt. Oreyo straightened his back and turned to her, walking over, and holding out his hand.

"May I have this dance?" he asked, and Laura knew what she had to do.

CHAPTER TWENTY EIGHT

Laura reached up her hand. "You may," she said, trying to take on the same kind of tone that he had – formal, polite, as if this was a real dance and not the twisted vision of a killer.

He took hold of her hand and hauled her to her feet in a way that was none too dignified, making her stumble and twist until he caught her in his arms. It was grotesque. Like a parody of something from an old romantic movie, but so far removed from it that it made her feel sick.

She didn't want a man who had already killed three women to put his arms around her. But then he shifted, drawing one of her hands out to the side with his own and helping her rest the other near his shoulder – not quite on it, given the restrictions of the ropes. His hands were cold and clammy. He supported her with an arm circling around her back, and then they were in position – the position they might take if they were really going to dance together.

And like that, he began to move.

Laura found herself dragged along with him, able to only control the very tips of her toes, trying desperately to balance and not fall as he took long and leisurely sweeps forward and back. There was no way for her to move her feet correctly to be able stabilize herself, not with them tied together as they were. She was at his mercy completely. That, she supposed, was probably the point.

"Your grandmother is sick," Laura said, a kind of guess. She didn't want to make it into a question, because if it was a question, he would know she knew nothing about the situation. She wanted him to think that she did. That was crucial, if her bluff was going to work.

"Yes," he admitted. "But not for long."

"Why is that?" Laura asked. In this case, she didn't think she could bluff that she knew what was going on inside his head. And though she suspected she might know the answer, she couldn't risk putting her foot in it and getting it wrong, which might anger him.

"Because I'm saving her," he said again. "I've already covered the rest of the song. You are the final one. Tonight, she will come home and everything will be back to normal."

It sounded like a mantra, like something he had been telling himself for weeks – or maybe even months. That was a very powerful thing. She wasn't going to be able to break it just by talking to him reasonably. It was a belief he was going to hold onto until the end. No, if she wanted this to work, she was going to have to try and discredit some other part of his plan. He had already shut down her insistence that she was the wrong person. What else was left?

"Are you sure it will work?" she asked, just to buy time so that she could think.

"I know it will," he said. A dreamy smile crossed his face, almost at odds with his sharp, gaunt features. "I've seen it already. She's improved so much every time. The doctor doesn't know what he's talking about."

"Which doctor is that?" Laura asked. They were approaching the end of the first chorus. It wasn't a long song. She knew that there was only the length of a few stanzas and then one more chorus to fade, and she would be out of time. If that was how it worked. She knew the song was still playing when they found the body, but... surely, if he wanted her found before the end, he ought to have killed her already?

But no... the rope burns. The other victims had them, and Laura could feel the material chafing against her skin with each awkward step. This dance was part of his normal ritual. It was what he always did with them.

Did he finish the song? Let it play again? How long would they have to do this for? There was no indication of how long any of the women had stayed with him before he killed them. A minute, an hour – they had no way of knowing. He could easily start the song again when she was dead.

"At the hospital," Oreyo frowned, as if he thought she ought to know that already. "The idiot one. He says she's going to die soon. From the dementia. But it's all going away. Tonight, she's going to come back home and she will be just fine. Even better than before."

"I see," Laura said. A plan was forming in her mind, a kind of Hail Mary. She wasn't even sure it would work. Maybe it would backfire spectacularly. But what choice did she have? If she did nothing, he was going to kill her. Might as well try something to change the outcome. "I have some bad news for you, Artur."

"What?" he snapped, his eyes going to hers with a speed that seemed somehow dangerous. Like he was just about to snap.

"It's about your grandmother," Laura said. "I was just coming back from the hospital when you saw me on the bridge."

"Why?" he asked. "Why were you at the hospital?"

"Because we were investigating you, of course," Laura said. She tried to keep her voice gentle and calm, so as not to set him off any further. She was weaving a lie from threads of the truth, trying to make him believe it. "Why do you think we came to your store?"

"She's fine," he said stubbornly. "Tonight everything will be better."

"I'm afraid it's too late," Laura said, and he stopped dancing as the final chorus of the song played, looking down at her. "I wish there was an easy way to say this, but there isn't. Artur, your grandmother passed away this afternoon."

It was such a gamble. There were any number of ways in which he might see through her story. Laura focused on remaining outwardly calm, using all of her training and experience to control her face, putting on that mask of authority that made people trust her as an FBI agent.

"No," he said. His grip on her arm tightened, squeezing so hard it hurt. "I was with her this afternoon."

"It was just after you left," Laura said. "She went downhill very quickly. They didn't have time to call you. I'm sure they tried to contact you at home, but you must have already gone out by then."

"She can't be dead," he said. "She was getting better."

"You didn't complete the circle," Laura said, using his own words back at him. "You didn't complete it, and now it's too late. You see, she was still vulnerable right up until the moment you finished your task. You didn't move fast enough."

"That can't be true," he hissed, his voice shaded with distress. "I did everything as fast as I could. I was just about to finish! You're the last one!"

"It was all a waste of effort," Laura said. "Everything you did – it was pointless. You couldn't do it fast enough to save her. It's too late, now. Nothing you do will make a difference. She's gone, and you can't bring her back even with the circle."

"You're lying," he said. He dropped her abruptly, sending her crashing to the floor. Laura managed to land on her side and her arm, avoiding a knock to the head or any serious damage, quickly shifting and bending her body so that she could look up at him again.

"I'm not lying," she insisted. "I know it's hard to hear, but she passed in the hospital. I'm sure the doctor told you how little time she had left. It just came sooner than expected."

"No." He turned, pacing away from her, rubbing his hand across his chin. Laura bent and arched quickly, trying to get into a better position to defend herself. "No, this is wrong. All wrong. She was getting better because of the others. She wouldn't suddenly die just like that."

"It must be terrible to hear," Laura said, trying to give him as much sympathy as she could. Trying to sound like she was there for him. "I'm sure you weren't expecting it."

"It's not true," he said. He turned, and his voice grew stronger. "It's not true. You're lying to me."

"I'm not lying," Laura insisted, but she could see on his face it was too late. The bluff had run out. He was calling her on it, and he was serious.

"You're a liar," he shot back, and she saw his face transform, going from worry and fear to pure anger. He opened his long jacket and pushed it aside, and then Laura saw what she hadn't before – the scabbard strapped to his side, lined up perfectly with his leg, the dark leather of it hidden easily in the length of his coat. The large stab wound they hadn't been able to figure out. It wasn't just a big knife.

He was using a sword.

And if she didn't get away from him...

CHAPTER TWENTY NINE

Nate raced into the warehouse with his gun drawn, only slowing down once he was close enough that he knew his footsteps would give him away. There was no use in getting himself caught, too. That wouldn't help Laura at all.

His own heartbeat was pounding in his ears as he stepped further inside, sweating in spite of the cold, his eyes darting in every direction. He had to get this right. It was likely he would only get one chance.

He almost tripped on a loose cable that was trailed across the floor, cursing himself inwardly but not daring to say anything out loud as he caught his balance. It had only made a small noise. There was a good chance the killer hadn't heard anything.

The fact that Nate couldn't hear any music – something that would have covered his entrance – was both a worry and a relief. A worry, because it might mean that he was in the wrong place. A relief, because if he was in the right place and the music wasn't playing yet, then Laura was still alive.

He'd already tried three different places. This had to be the one. It had to be.

Goddamn Dean still hadn't called him back, and there were far too many warehouses and abandoned places to check by himself. He could have called the local cops, but he didn't trust them to do it right. Didn't have time to give them full instructions. He needed to find Laura by instinct, and this warehouse had looked like a good place to hide up with a victim you really, really wouldn't want to get away.

An FBI agent. He had to know that if she survived, he was going to prison for a very long time. He had to know. And because he knew, he wasn't going to let her get out of here alive if he could help it. He would kill at the first chance he got.

The only thing Nate could rely on, the thing that was making him sweat not quite enough for the gun to slip through his fingers, was the fact that he had this weird-ass ritual to follow. Maybe he would get distracted by that for long enough that Nate could actually get this done. Find Laura. Shoot the bad guy. Get her out of there.

There was a sound – something up ahead.

Nate froze to listen, the grip of the gun warm under his hand as it adjusted to his body temperature. He felt like he could hear the seconds ticking by, and then – yes, there it was again! A human voice, he thought, though he couldn't be sure. It was coming from somewhere up ahead. The warehouse was almost completely dark, shrouded in half-fallen old plastic curtain dividers and rotting piles of crates, water dripping from a few holes in the ceiling from where it must have rained last. But somewhere up there...

Nate inched forward slowly until he could hear it better. Someone was... humming? Yes – humming! Someone was humming out there, low under their breath. Some kind of tune.

Nate's hand tensed on the grip of his gun as he realized they must be closer than he thought. He couldn't see anything, but the humming – for him to hear it this clearly...

He stepped forward, taking care with every single step, agonizingly slow. What he really wanted to do was to burst forward and tell the guy to put his hands above his head, make him stop whatever he was doing. But he had to be cautious. Had to remind himself.

So long as the music isn't playing, Laura's alive.

Unless, of course, the killer had decided that she wasn't worthy of his ritual and just killed her anyway. And was now standing over her corpse as her lifeblood spread out across the warehouse floor, humming gently to himself...

Nate gritted his teeth and took another step, refusing to allow this vision of darkness to take over. He couldn't let it get to him. Couldn't panic. If he did, it was definitely over for Laura, whether the killer had made his move yet or not.

Another step.

Nate leaned carefully around a stack of crates, piled above the height of his head, trying to see. He froze and darted back again, holding his breath, trying hard not to gasp or give himself away by any other noise. There was someone there.

Cautiously and slowly, Nate leaned forward again. The figure – it was a man, he thought – was sitting with his back to Nate. He was on the floor in what seemed to be a random spot amongst the detritus of the former warehouse, his back arched over in a curve. No, not sitting – crouching, resting on his haunches. In front of him there was something big and dark, something covering the floor...

Laura?

The visibility was bad. Nate couldn't see a thing. Had no way of knowing if the guy had a knife or some other weapon in his hand. And the humming... the *humming*. It was low and persistent, eerie in the abandoned space, echoing slightly around them. It put a shiver down Nate's spine. Exactly the way that a deranged killer might.

He had two choices here. Keep creeping forward until he could see better and hope he wouldn't disturb the guy, which would be near impossible since he might have to be right on him to see anything. Or make a stand right now and hope that he wasn't putting Laura in further danger.

A drop of sweat slid down Nate's forehead, trailing off to the side and going past his eye.

He had to make a choice.

It was now or never.

"Freeze!" he shouted, using the full force and loudness of his voice, keeping the gun steady in front of him. "Stay where you are and slowly put your hands above your head!"

The humming stopped abruptly. The guy swayed on his haunches, almost going down, his back going tight with tension. Slowly, very slowly, two hands appeared and rose through the air, heading for the ceiling.

"Don't move," Nate barked, moving forward, keeping the gun trained on him as he began to circle around to the front. "Stay right where you are."

There was no response. He came around to a position where he could see the guy's face and blinked. He was young – younger than Nate had expected. In the dim light it was hard to see, but he thought his face was dirty. He looked down at the ground for a single glance, at the dark shape on the ground.

Not a person.

It was a collection of things – a duffel bag at one end, some spread-out materials that looked like maybe blankets or towels, what looked in the poor light like a bunch of clothes. A collection of belongings. Nate looked at the guy again.

He was wide-eyed, looking up at Nate with a gaze that seemed luminous in the darkness. Nate looked again. His pupils were blown.

Nate grabbed a flashlight and shone it down at the floor and saw what he was really looking at. Not a killer. Not a psycho kidnapper who had taken Laura.

A kid who was sleeping rough and probably high on something to help him deal with it.

"Shit!" Nate swore. "Kid, you seen anyone else around here? Anyone at all?"

The kid shook his head slowly side to side. His hands were still up in the air. He looked as though he'd taken the instruction to freeze quite literally. Like he was afraid to breathe in case his chest rising and falling counted as moving.

Nate let out a groan of total frustration and fear, turning to kick out at another length of cable that had been left abandoned on the floor of the warehouse. He was in the wrong place.

He turned and left the kid, running back the way he had come, knowing it was now that much more likely that Laura would be dead before he even got there.

***

There was a kind of swish as Oreyo drew the sword from its scabbard. Laura saw that it was wickedly sharp, and even without knowing he had already used it to kill three women, she would have known she was in trouble. It glinted in the dim light of the place, and when Oreyo let the point thump against the ground, it was an even more noticeable noise in the absence of the song. The gramophone was silent, and Laura wondered if that made a difference.

"You can't kill me," she said. "The song."

"If my grandmother is dead, I don't need the song," he snarled at her, his upper lip curling. "And if she's not dead, then I don't need *you*. I can find someone else. You're disposable."

Laura swallowed hard at the sound of the word. He advanced towards her fast, too fast, leaving her without enough time to think and consider her next move. No time to say something else to distract him. She threw herself to one side, rolling away from him –

And rolling to her feet, using the momentum to propel her without the use of her hands. She'd managed to get the ropes loose while he had his back turned, finishing off the work she had started before he knew she was awake. Oreyo crashed forward towards the ground where she had been laying and almost fell, catching his balance at the last minute with the heavy sword still in his hand. Laura dodged backwards, further away from him. They were in a big space. She needed to use that to her advantage as much as she could. She needed to keep him at a distance as much as possible. Out of the reach of that sword.

He swung it at her again and Laura gasped, dodging it only by the virtue of sucking in her stomach and leaning her body, far too close for comfort. She picked up the pace, stumbling backwards, knowing that if she lost her balance or tripped it would be over.

She'd seen this movie a dozen times. She knew what was going to happen. Sooner or later in her mad stumble, she would collide with something she hadn't known was there and fly backwards – or she'd hit her back against the wall and be left with nowhere else to go. It was inevitable.

She needed to change the dynamic before it reached that point.

He swung towards her again and missed, and Laura took advantage of the moment – of the weight of the sword forcing him to regroup before he could make another move – to turn.

She assessed the space in a heartbeat, adding to what she had already seen when she was on the floor. The door was behind her, behind Oreyo, and there was no way past him. But at the back of the room there was a large stack of wooden pallets, no doubt left there from when the warehouse was in use. She ran towards it, full speed, knowing that he was at a disadvantage while he still had to carry the heavy weapon.

She was running for her life and that fact made her feet fast. Laura made it to the space behind the pallets and didn't waste a moment. Instead of waiting for him to round the corner after her, she simply pushed – pushed as hard as she could against the whole stack of pallets, taller than she was, until they started to fall.

There was an almighty clatter as the stack toppled. Not only did they fall, but they were so old that many of them were rotten, snapping and creaking as they went down. A cloud of dust rose up into the air, choking her and filling her mouth as she took advantage of the moment to continue running instead of checking whether she had managed to hit him. The door was on the other side of the room. If she made it, she could be free. She could run and hide somewhere else, outpace him, find someone to flag down for help.

She almost tripped, caught partway between dodging to the side and stopping completely, when someone filled the doorway.

For a moment her heart stuttered a desperate fear that Oreyo had not been working alone, that she had calculated wrong, that it was all going to end now.

139

But then she recognized that shape, that silhouette outlined against the doorway, and she knew she was safe.

"Freeze!" Nate yelled, pointing the gun behind her as she made it the last few steps to his side, his firearm over her shoulder. "Stop right there or I'll shoot!"

Laura turned and saw him, Artur Oreyo, stuttering to a halt behind her. He had been only steps away. His dark outfit was now coated in dust, and one of his sleeves was torn where the pallets had come down on him. There was even dust in his hair, and he was breathing hard. The sword was still in his hand, though it pointed downward, dragging against the ground.

"You're under arrest for attempted murder of an FBI agent," Nate growled. "And three homicides. Drop the sword and put your hands above your head."

"No," Oreyo said, and before Laura could get over the shock of his refusal, he swung desperately and fast with the sword, hitting Nate's gun.

It fell to the floor and skittered away harmlessly, and Laura's breath caught in her throat.

They were unarmed, and Oreyo was still advancing.

CHAPTER THIRTY

Nate stumbled backwards, clutching at his hand with the other, taking Laura with him by accident in the circle of his arms. He let go as she turned, everything seeming to happen so slowly as the adrenaline surged through his veins.

"Go!" Laura breathed, and she was on her way already, her feet pushing off the ground to give her a head start, and Nate saw Oreyo lifting his sword for another swing and knew she was right. They had to go.

Nate launched himself after Laura as fast as he could, only narrowly avoiding another swing of the sword. It was heavy, clunking hard against the frame of the door and sticking there for a moment as Oreyo fought to draw it back. That was the only thing that saved them, Nate watching as he ran backwards to make sure they had enough headway before turning to run faster.

Laura was just ahead of him. He outpaced her easily, given his longer legs, but he didn't outstrip her. He stayed level at her side, knowing he had that extra tank he could call on if things got desperate, not willing to let her be the person bringing up the rear. The person right in the firing line for that sword if it came down again.

"Come on," Nate said, urging her onwards. "This whole complex of warehouses is abandoned. We just need to get in somewhere ahead of him and hide."

"I'm trying," Laura gasped, already heavily out of breath.

Nate glanced at her and then over his shoulder again. Oreyo was following them, running slower with the sword at his side but starting to gather steam. It was the look of determination on his face that put a chill down Nate's spine. He looked like he would rather drop dead himself than allow them to get away. That kind of psychotic determination might last much longer than either he or Laura could run for, and this area of town was so isolated...

And Laura was flagging already. She looked sick. She'd been taken by the killer, and she wouldn't have gone down without a fight. Nate reasoned she must be hurt already. He needed to get her to safety.

Marsters had called him back with the cell trace, leading him right to the warehouse he'd found her in, when he was already close by. Marsters knew where they were. All he had to do was ask Marsters to call in for backup...

They plunged together into the darkness of another warehouse, both of them staggering for a moment, brought up sharp by the sheer blackness that embraced them. With no light from outside and thick, heavy walls surrounding them, they might as well have fallen down a well.

"Hold on," Nate whispered, grabbing Laura's arm as she tried to go in the direction of one of the windows where light entered from a position near the moon. "This way."

He had the advantage of knowing that this warehouse was very like the one he had explored before, where he had come across the homeless kid. It was in the same condition. Rotting crates, plastic sheeting that was halfway through the process of falling down, the odd puddle of standing water where a hole in the ceiling let it in. And Nate knew that if this warehouse was the same, hiding would be easy. They just had to find a spot where they couldn't be seen, keep an ear out for approaching footsteps, and then...

But the footsteps came far too soon – or, rather, the sound of metal dragging. Nate was just leading Laura, pulling her by the arm, towards a tall stack of rotting crates that might hide them when he heard it. Oreyo was entering the warehouse. He was still close behind them, even with the weight of the sword dragging across the floor. His footsteps were covered by the light symphony of dripping water from the various holes in the roof, and Nate hoped their footsteps were as well, but the sword scratched through it all like nails on a chalkboard. Laura stumbled against Nate and made a small noise as he caught her, and Nate's own breath caught in his throat. If Oreyo heard...

Sure enough, the scraping sword seemed to turn in their direction. Nate changed target, fixing his eyes ahead of the stack. There was a length of plastic sheeting that seemed to reach across half the warehouse, only just visible as a vague outline in the darkness. Behind that, somewhere, there would be another place to hide. They had to keep going. Had to put as many layers between them and Oreyo as possible.

Nate focused on moving quietly and carefully, dropping speed in favor of not tripping over anything. Laura was lagging, leaning heavily against his arm now, her feet beginning to drag against the ground.

Nate could feel her exhaustion. He gritted his teeth. He needed to be strong for both of them.

"There."

It was a whisper, so quiet he almost didn't hear it, fixed right into his ear. But he did hear it, and when he followed Laura's gaze he saw. There were two more sheets of plastic flapping loosely from rails on the ceiling, and behind them, another tall stack of crates. Two stacks, side by side. Perfect to shield them from Oreyo's detection. And best of all, they were at a diagonal angle across the warehouse from their current position, a line that Oreyo might not expect them to take.

Nate redoubled his efforts, the sound of that metallic scraping ringing in his ears and seeming to fill his entire head, desperate to make it there before some errant shaft of light from a passing car would illuminate them for Oreyo's eyes.

He made it behind the crates, pulling Laura with him, and found himself slumping down on the floor as quietly as he could. He was breathing hard and trying to stifle it at the same time, the effort of getting away while also supporting Laura's weight having taken its toll on him. She sat beside him, resting, but her head lolled on her neck.

"Laura?" he asked, risking a ghost of a whisper. The sound of the scraping was continuing, but it sounded further away. Far enough that they might be able to communicate.

"My head," she murmured back, not a whisper and yet somehow quieter than his had been. "He hit me over the head."

"Shit." Nate moved quietly to glance around the stack of crates. He caught a glimpse of light flashing off something long and thin: the sword. Oreyo was across the other side of the warehouse, still following the path he and Laura had originally set off on. They had fooled him, but only for now. Sooner or later he would get to the end of the space and realize he had missed them, and then he would come look for them. With Laura so tired and obviously reeling, Nate didn't know how long they could keep running. She must have used up all the energy she had in trying to get away before he arrived.

They needed help.

Nate grabbed his cell phone and turned, putting it inside his coat and using it as a shield around the phone, stopping too much light from spilling out. Even so, when he turned on the screen it made his heart pound in his chest even faster. It seemed so bright in the darkness of the warehouse. A telltale sign, if Oreyo looked around. Nate hit the

143

brightness slider and put it all the way down, but it wasn't enough. He needed to do this quick.

There was no chance of making a call. He typed out a quick message to Marsters – *HIDING FROM KILLER. TRACE L FROST CELL & MY CELL. BACKUP REQUIRED URGENTLY.* Then another to Captain Kinnock, hoping he would be fast enough and careful enough to actually help – *ABANDONED WAREHOUSE COMPLEX ABOVE TINNERY BRIDGE – KILLER WITH SWORD – BACKUP REQUIRED URGENTLY – AGENTS UNARMED.*

He thought about sending another message or two to Kinnock to try and explain more in case the man didn't get it, but he was relying more on the FBI resources at any rate. It wasn't worth the risk of keeping the light of the screen on. Marsters would send someone – he could rely on that. Nate turned off the screen and tucked the phone back into his pocket, making doubly sure to turn the volume slider to silent as he did so. They couldn't have a phone call or a message alert giving them away, not now.

"Just hold on," Nate whispered, so quiet it was almost under his breath. "Help's coming."

Laura said nothing, but she pressed a hand against his arm in the darkness – a gesture of understanding and reassurance both. He patted her hand back with his own: message received.

Sudden silence made Nate sit up straight, his hand automatically going for his gun belt and closing on empty air in the absence of the weapon.

The sound of the sword scraping on the floor was gone.

Was Oreyo standing still somewhere?

Or had he picked up the blade so that he could approach them silently?

***

Laura's head pounded and she rubbed at her temples, trying to get it to stop. The pain was so bad, she was having trouble keeping upright. It must have been the exertion. The pain had faded away when she was lying still on the floor, going down to a more manageable level. But since she'd got up and tried to run away, it had become so much worse. She had to have a concussion. That would be it.

But it wasn't like she didn't have experience dealing with bad headaches. Wasn't like she didn't know how to push through them.

144

She needed to think. That was the problem. Thinking through the pain.

"Just hold on," Nate whispered. "Help's coming."

Laura nodded in the darkness and flinched, feeling the pain roll through her head at the movement. She reached out and squeezed his arm lightly to let him know she'd understood. She would hold on. Nate reached up to touch her hand back, another wordless gesture.

And a wave of darkness washed over her, so thick she thought she was going to throw up there and then –

Nate was sitting right there when the blade sliced through the side of the stack of crates and through his body, making him choke up red blood that looked black in the darkness –

Laura came back to herself as she wrenched her hand away from Nate's, taking in a huge gasping breath. He swung around to look at her, and Laura realized then what was wrong – the silence. Oreyo had gone quiet. She couldn't hear the sound of the blade any longer.

He was coming.

"We have to get out," she whispered urgently, her voice ragged around the edges, and Nate must have understood she'd had a vision or maybe just trusted her enough to do whatever she asked, because within the space of a second he was on his feet and reaching down for her. She grabbed his arm and pulled herself up, the adrenaline taking over again, the pressure of a vision on top of the headache she already had somehow working in the opposite direction and giving her lightness that lifted her out of the pain and into total clarity.

They had to run.

Even now, somewhere, Oreyo was circling around, approaching their position, getting ready to strike. He must have seen the light. He knew where they were.

Laura moved ahead of Nate now, gaining confidence in each step. The headache was gone. She could see the doorway up ahead, a slice of the outside world, a sky with stars more visible the closer they got towards it. A street. They just had to get out there.

She knew she could change the future that her visions showed her. She knew she'd saved Nate's life once by pulling him out of the place where the blade would slice in perhaps just a few moments. But there was still a risk. There was still the chance of a new future in which Oreyo caught up with them anyway, slashed out, caught Nate with the sword or even her –

There was a crashing noise behind them and Laura jumped almost out of her own skin, starting to run by instinct. Nate was right at her side. Her brain processed the noise as the clattering of the stack of crates coming down, no doubt after Oreyo had plunged his sword through them and into nothingness, not finding Nate where he had expected to find him. He let out a shout of rage, and Laura knew then that they had to keep running as fast as they could, because Oreyo wasn't about to let them get away.

"Come on!" she called, putting on a burst of speed and glancing aside to make sure Nate was keeping up with her. Just a little bit further – just a short distance to the freedom of the outside – she hit the doorway and sped through it, feeling the difference in the open sky above her almost immediately.

The cold night air hitting her hot skin told her how much exertion she had put in, how deeply the fear was hitting her. She turned her steps towards the road, racing across a wide expanse of concrete that must have once served as a loading bay for the warehouse. Nate was right beside her. She chanced another look over her shoulder and regretted it: Oreyo was there, framed in the doorway, the sword up in his arms as he charged at full pelt after them.

They could beat him in raw speed over an open space like this. They had even rested, and he hadn't. Laura felt stronger now, clearer since her vision. They just had to stay ahead of him. They just had to stay ahead until they reached help. Laura tumbled towards the edge of the loading bay, turning around the corner of a neighboring warehouse, getting a clear view of the road –

And the sirens blasted out as the three police cars screeched up towards her, allowing Laura and Nate to run past their steaming grilles and their blazing headlights to the relative safety behind them, officers jumping out of both sides of each car to raise guns and point them at Oreyo.

"Drop your weapon!" one of them shouted, and Laura recognized the voice of Captain Kinnock. "Put it on the ground and raise your hands above your head! Do it *now!*"

Laura fought for breath as she watched Oreyo drop the sword with a clatter that resounded from the concrete. Nate was safe beside her, panting heavily, both his and her breath making clouds of white in the air around them. Laura reached out to touch him, grabbing his arm and then his hand. Making sure he was whole. Making sure the shadow of death no longer had hold of him. He was clean.

It was over.

They'd survived – and Artur Oreyo's reign of terror was over.

CHAPTER THIRTY ONE

The sound of hammering at the door jolted Laura awake. She opened her eyes and looked at the door in fear, instinct making her shrink back on the bed.

"Laura!" Nate yelled from outside. "Laura, are you alright?"

She swallowed, trying to assess herself. She didn't even know the answer to the question. "Yes," she hazarded, thinking that there were no outward signs to the contrary.

"Jesus." There was the sound of him slumping, leaning against the motel room door. "You were screaming again."

"Sorry." Laura pressed a hand against her forehead. She didn't even remember it this time, but she would have bet good money on what she must have been dreaming about. Zach and Chris, again. She glanced at the clock. She'd only been asleep for three hours. "I'm really sorry. Just go back to sleep."

"I'm awake now," Nate said. "How about you?"

Laura tried to think past the confusion and the fact that she'd been asleep a minute before. "Are you asking me if we should just head home?"

"Pretty much," Nate said, his voice still muffled by the door. "We said we'd just get a few hours of sleep and then drive back, after all."

"Sure," Laura replied, sitting up properly in the bed and moving her limbs to get them woken up. "You know I wanted to go out right away anyway. I only agreed to a nap because you were too tired to drive."

Nate snorted. "Yeah, alright," he said. "Be at the car in ten?"

"Ten it is," Laura agreed, throwing the covers back.

"Alright." Nate's footsteps moved off outside, past her window, and then she heard the door of the neighboring room open and shut.

She took a breath. What a way to wake up. And for poor Nate, too. She hoped to God he wasn't going to ask her what she'd been dreaming about so often.

She dressed and grabbed her things fast, a practiced routine that she had gotten down to a fine art, and unlocked the car exactly eight minutes after Nate had walked away from her room. He joined her not thirty seconds later, nodding that he was ready as she reached for the door handle. Over his head, it looked like dawn wasn't far off from breaking.

"Are you sure you're alright for the drive?" Nate asked. He paused to wait for her answer, looking her over with his own hand poised to open the door.

"I'll be fine," Laura said. She gave him a small smile. "You're the one who needs to be alert enough not to send us into a five-car pileup, anyway."

"Right," Nate said, shaking his head with a chuckle as he climbed into the driver's side.

Laura slumped beside him in the passenger seat and watched as he entered their destination into the GPS. "Just three hours to go until we're home."

"Until we're back at HQ," Nate corrected her. "A little while more than that for home."

"Right," Laura sighed. She closed her eyes for a moment, nestling against the seat, then looked at him. "Want to debrief from last night?"

"Good idea," Nate agreed, his voice a low grunt. After they had made the arrest, had Laura checked over by the medics to make sure there were no lasting effects from the sedative, and then done the paperwork to get Oreyo booked in formally, they'd been tired enough to just go straight to bed. "I reached our rendezvous point and found your car, but no you. I figured then what must have happened. I was right about the killer being at your bridge."

"No need to rub it in," Laura said. "How did you know where he'd taken me?"

"I got Dean Marsters to track your cell phone," Nate said. "I couldn't get an exact hit, obviously, - once you were inside the warehouse the signal was even worse. But Dean sent me the map of the area and it only covered a couple of warehouses, one of which was way too broken down to be of use to anyone. I figured out that he must have taken you to the one spot that fit the bill."

"Smart," Laura said.

Nate cast a sideways look in her direction. "Actually, to be honest, that was the third or fourth property I checked. There are a lot of empty buildings in that part of town. I had already called Captain Kinnock to send his guys to check out a ton more, too. That's how they got to us so fast after I sent the SOS message."

Laura chuckled. "Well, I'm glad to know you had the perseverance to keep going."

"I wasn't going to just leave you," Nate said. There was still a hint of the joking tone they'd had before, but something more serious underlined his words. Like he wanted her to know it for sure. "Anyway. I guess we don't always need your visions to solve cases, huh?"

Laura sighed, looking out of the window. "Sorry," she said. "I wish I'd been more helpful."

"More helpful than finding the killer?" Nate's voice was reproachful. "Laura, you still solved the case. It was you who was convinced we had the wrong man – and you who figured out the bridge. And you did actually save my life, remember? Anyway, I'm kind of relieved."

"Relieved?" Laura frowned, turning back to look at him. "Why?"

"Because I'd started to think we actually weren't all that good at solving cases, and we only managed it due to your visions," Nate said, drumming his fingers lightly on the steering wheel. They were heading out onto the highway, away from the town. "Now I know I am actually a good agent, and we can figure it out without any of your voodoo."

"It's not voodoo," Laura chuckled. She turned what he'd said over in her mind. She hadn't realized he had felt that way still. "But you're a great agent, Nate. One of the best. I could have told you that."

"It's nice to have it confirmed," he said.

They rested in silence for a while, the miles beginning to tick away under the wheels of the car. Even though she felt restless and constrained in the vehicle, Laura knew it wasn't so long now until they would get back. Not like in other cases when they'd been on the other side of the country. There was that to be grateful for, at least.

"I still can't believe it," Laura sighed. "About his grandmother."

Nate shook his head. "You really didn't know?" he asked. "I thought for sure it must have been something you'd seen before I got there, when you said you'd told him that."

"No, I had no idea," Laura said. "I didn't even know there *was a* grandmother until he accidentally let it slip. And to think she died all alone in that hospital while he was trying to kill me."

"Poor kid," Nate muttered.

Laura shot him a sideways glance. "He killed three people and tried to murder me."

"I know," Nate said. "But he did it because someone he loved was dying and he didn't know how to cope. It's messed up. But I still feel for him, you know? If only someone could have shown him the way to deal with it properly. It sounds like he never had much of a stable childhood."

"Yeah." Laura watched the scenery flashing by on the side of the road and thought of Lacey. Lacey, split between two homes, always sharing her time between her father and mother. She hoped she was going to grow up to feel she had love and support from two families, rather than one that was broken. "I guess the undiagnosed schizophrenia in his grandmother had a big part to play. That kind of thing can run in families. I think he was sick – sick for a long time. Maybe his mother was, too, before she died. He needed proper help a long time ago."

There was a little silence while they both considered it. It was a bad situation made worse by circumstances. The difference in Oreyo getting help at a younger age and the way he had turned out now was enormous. Lives had been lost, and it could all have been prevented by proper mental health treatment for both him and his grandmother. And perhaps the intervention of social services to take him away from a household that was ultimately abusive and violent.

"You can go back to sleep, if you want," Nate offered. "I'm doing fine. I can manage to get us back in one piece."

"Hmm." Laura nestled a little further into her seat and yawned. It wasn't her usual style, but…

Maybe just this once.

***

Laura wandered through her empty apartment in bare feet, enjoying the feeling of being dressed in jeans and a plain t-shirt for once. It wasn't often she got the chance to sit around doing nothing on a weekday. Normally it was because she was off work for medical reasons, ordered by Chief Rondelle to stay at home, but this time she actually felt fine. He and Nate were being far too cautious about making her take time off, given the fact the sedative had worn off pretty quickly.

Still, having a day off to herself was pretty nice, as it happened.

She grabbed a half loaf of bread from the counter and checked, pleasantly surprised to find that it hadn't gone bad yet. All she needed was some kind of filling and she was on her way to a sandwich.

There was a knock at the door which made her frown and pause. She wasn't expecting anyone today. Nate was in the office doing paperwork, and besides, he would let her know he was coming ahead of time. Maybe a delivery – though she didn't recall ordering anything.

She moved to the door and looked through the peephole, and immediately clasped her hand over her mouth to stop herself from giving away her presence by making any noise. Maybe if he didn't know she was there, he would go away.

Zach knocked loudly again, and Laura groaned inwardly. He was a psychic like her, after all. For all she knew, he'd already seen she was home in a vision.

Besides, he'd been trying to get in touch with her for days. If she just let him in now, when she knew that Chris wasn't going to be anywhere near her, maybe that would be alright. Then she could put off meeting him for another while to prevent their paths from ever crossing.

She opened the door, trying her very best to smile at Zach instead of grimacing. "Hi," she said.

"Hello!" Zach answered cheerfully, breezing past her quickly and pushing his way into the apartment. "I've been trying to get ahold of you."

Laura turned with wide eyes, wondering how he'd managed to get the jump on her that quickly and just make his way inside. It was something to do with his grandfatherly manner – you didn't expect it from him.

"Zach," she said. "I've only just come back from working a case. I'm supposed to be on medical leave."

He turned and looked her over with concern. She hadn't closed the front door. "Are you alright?"

"Well, yes, I'm fine," Laura said, struggling with the instinct to not lie and the fact that she didn't want him to stay for long if it could be helped. "I'm quite tired. Is there something that you wanted to talk about?"

"I won't keep you long," he said. "I just wanted to ask about your visions. Have you been getting them lately?"

Laura closed the door quickly and stepped away from it, not wanting any of her neighbors to overhear the way he was talking. "I don't know," she said, which was obviously a stupid and confusing response and wouldn't help to make it sound like she was telling the truth. She amended herself immediately. "I mean, I've been getting dreams. I don't know yet whether they're visions or not."

"I've had a few dreams myself," Zach said. "No new visions though, not since we last spoke. It's the same as how you described. It seems to be getting worse."

"I don't know what's causing it," Laura sighed. As much as she wanted some time to herself, it was true that they needed to get to the bottom of this. The whole reason she had allowed contact with Zach in the first place was because she wanted to understand her ability better. Now that this was happening... she needed to find the answers. Working together was the only way they could get even remotely close to doing that.

"I've been thinking," Zach said. "I have two possibilities. The first is that my visions led me to you because this was going to happen, and the only way we can solve it is by working together. The other option is that we're causing it ourselves *by* being close to one another. Maybe there's some kind of interference caused by our interactions that's stopping the visions from getting through."

"We should test it," Laura said, seizing on that idea immediately. "We should go complete no contact for a few weeks and see what happens. And I mean nothing – no calls, no texts. We don't speak at all. We'll check in with one another on – what, the same date exactly a month from now?"

"That sounds fair," Zach said, tilting his head from one side to the other. "I'm not sure it will work, mind you, but it's worth trying. A scientific method. I like your approach!"

"Thanks," Laura said, almost absent-mindedly. She was just focused now on getting him out of the apartment. Of making sure that she didn't need to worry about him meeting Chris for at least another month – and maybe further beyond that, if it turned out that the second option was right. "Well, I'll contact you in a month, then." She re-opened the door, gesturing through it as an indication that it was time for him to leave.

"Oh," Zach said, looking up into the doorway.

Laura turned her head and her heart nearly plummeted through the floor.

"Hi," Chris said, looking between her and Zach hesitantly. "Is this a bad time?"

Laura could hardly speak. It was happening. All she'd done to avoid it, and it was happening.

Chris was holding a takeout container in his hands. He'd come to surprise her with lunch. She'd told him about the medical leave, and he must have decided to come over.

And now, despite all her best efforts – she was going to lose them both.

"Not at all, not at all," Zach said. "I was just on my way out. Looks like you two are about to have a splendid lunch!"

Chris grinned at that, stepping in through the door and then to one side in order to let Zach out. Zach passed by him, nodding at Laura. She felt frozen, like she couldn't do or say anything. She had no idea how to stop this from happening. All she knew was that somehow, at some point, this situation was going to go from smiles and handshakes to the most violent end possible.

"Well, I'll speak to you in a month, then, like we said," Zach told her, smiling benevolently. Laura almost cringed. Was that it? Was Chris going to be jealous now? She swallowed down bile, trying to breathe.

"Oh?" Chris asked, polite casualness, looking between him and Laura. "What's in a month?"

"Building committee meeting," Zach said, still wearing that same smile. He lied easily, Laura thought. Too easily. What else had he lied about? "I'm one of Laura's neighbors here. We've got some improvements coming up and we like to involve as many of the residents as possible."

"Right," Chris nodded, smiling back at him. "Well, good luck."

Zach nodded at Laura one more time and started to walk away, smile still on his face. Laura only saw it falter for a moment as he took that first step. For a moment, she cursed him. What if Chris had seen that happen? She went to close the door –

But something was wrong. Zach had clutched his hand across his chest, staggering to one side instead of continuing to walk straight on.

"Zach?" Laura said, opening the door wider again.

He was falling to his knees.

Chris rushed forwards, out into the hall, and he set his briefcase down on the floor beside Zach, rapidly grabbing hold of him. "Can you hear me?" he asked. "Can you tell me what you're feeling?"

Zach only made a choking noise, but he managed to gesture to his arm and his chest, his face going red. He fell down to the floor, laying out flat –

Laying out like Laura had seen in her dream.

154

Chris thrust his briefcase open and rifled through it, the lid of it open towards Laura so that she couldn't see what he was doing.

She had seen this so many times. Zach on the floor. Chris over him. Adrenaline took over. She didn't even think. She couldn't let this happen. She couldn't let Chris kill him. Whatever he was taking out of the briefcase was –

The knife –

She pulled her gun, pointing it at Chris. "No!" she yelled desperately, forgetting all of her training in an instant, forgetting to be clear and give directions, only knowing that she needed to make him stop.

Chris stared at her, pausing, frozen still as though she'd managed to stop time. Zach was moving, but only a little. He was still making that choking noise.

"Is he allergic?" Chris demanded, reaching into the briefcase again. His other hand was visible now beyond the edge of it. He was holding a syringe.

Laura stared back at him.

"Laura?" he barked, every inch the medical professional, needing the quick answer so that he could save a life.

"I don't know," she breathed, dropping the gun by her side.

Chris turned, ignoring her now and focused on Zach, and used one hand to hold him still. "Just hold on," he told the other man, and then his hand came down, plunging the needle through Zach's chest and releasing the plunger.

There was a tense moment, and then Zach gasped for breath, color slowly returning to normal in his face.

"Call 911," Chris instructed Laura, still not looking at her. "He still needs to go to hospital and get checked out. He's just had a heart attack."

Laura fumbled to holster her gun, reaching for her cell phone instead. She opened it and dialed automatically, and when the dispatched asked for details she said them like she was reading them from a piece of paper. Ambulance, her home address, heart attack, given shot of – Chris told her it was adrenaline. The dispatcher said that help was on the way. Laura put her phone in her pocket.

Everything was happening so slowly and yet far too fast. She didn't know if she'd taken a breath since Zach fell to the ground. It was like her body was trapped in treacle. She didn't even know if she would be able to take a step or if she'd just fall over.

"The ambulance is on its way, sir," Chris said, reassuring Zach as he folded up his coat and put it under his head for support. "You just hold tight until then. We'll have you in great condition in no time."

"Th-thank you," Zach managed to say breathlessly.

"Don't thank me. Just stay still and don't try to talk," Chris instructed him. "Help will be here soon, but don't stress yourself out until then."

"Alright," Zach replied hoarsely. He leaned his head down on the jacket and seemed to relax, looking up at the ceiling.

"And then, when the ambulance has come and gone," Chris said, looking at Laura. "We can talk about what the hell that was."

Laura swallowed hard, taking a step back inside the apartment.

She'd screwed up.

And she had no idea how she was going to explain any of this.

NOW AVAILABLE!

ALREADY HIS
(A Laura Frost FBI Suspense Thriller—Book 9)

FBI Special Agent Laura Frost is summoned to a mysterious crime scene: a victim has been left tied to a carved, wooden figurehead from an old ship—the second such victim in two weeks. What is the symbolism behind this killer's signature? And can her psychic gift lead her to the answer?

"A masterpiece of thriller and mystery."
—Books and Movie Reviews, Roberto Mattos (re Once Gone)

ALREADY HIS (A Laura Frost FBI Suspense Thriller) is book #9 in a long-anticipated new series by #1 bestseller and USA Today bestselling author Blake Pierce, whose bestseller Once Gone (a free download) has received over 1,000 five star reviews. The Laura Frost series begins with ALREADY GONE (Book #1).

FBI Special Agent and single mom Laura Frost, 35, is haunted by her talent: a psychic ability which she refuses to face and which she keeps secret from her colleagues. While Laura gets obscured glimpses of what the killer may do next, she must decide whether to trust her confusing gift—or her investigative work.

The figurehead is rife with ancient myth and symbolism, and any of the lore might be the driving motive behind this killer's warped M.O.

But entering his mind is the only way to find out—and that is the one thing Laura does not want to do.

A page-turning and harrowing crime thriller featuring a brilliant and tortured FBI agent, the LAURA FROST series is a startlingly fresh mystery, rife with suspense, twists and turns, shocking revelations, and driven by a breakneck pace that will keep you flipping pages late into the night.

Future books in the series will be available soon.

"An edge of your seat thriller in a new series that keeps you turning pages! ...So many twists, turns and red herrings... I can't wait to see what happens next."
—Reader review (Her Last Wish)

"A strong, complex story about two FBI agents trying to stop a serial killer. If you want an author to capture your attention and have you guessing, yet trying to put the pieces together, Pierce is your author!"
—Reader review (Her Last Wish)

"A typical Blake Pierce twisting, turning, roller coaster ride suspense thriller. Will have you turning the pages to the last sentence of the last chapter!!!"
—Reader review (City of Prey)

"Right from the start we have an unusual protagonist that I haven't seen done in this genre before. The action is nonstop... A very atmospheric novel that will keep you turning pages well into the wee hours."
—Reader review (City of Prey)

"Everything that I look for in a book... a great plot, interesting characters, and grabs your interest right away. The book moves along at a breakneck pace and stays that way until the end. Now on go I to book two!"
—Reader review (Girl, Alone)

"Exciting, heart pounding, edge of your seat book... a must read for mystery and suspense readers!"
—Reader review (Girl, Alone)

Blake Pierce

Blake Pierce is the USA Today bestselling author of the RILEY PAGE mystery series, which includes seventeen books. Blake Pierce is also the author of the MACKENZIE WHITE mystery series, comprising fourteen books; of the AVERY BLACK mystery series, comprising six books; of the KERI LOCKE mystery series, comprising five books; of the MAKING OF RILEY PAIGE mystery series, comprising six books; of the KATE WISE mystery series, comprising seven books; of the CHLOE FINE psychological suspense mystery, comprising six books; of the JESSE HUNT psychological suspense thriller series, comprising twenty four books; of the AU PAIR psychological suspense thriller series, comprising three books; of the ZOE PRIME mystery series, comprising six books; of the ADELE SHARP mystery series, comprising sixteen books, of the EUROPEAN VOYAGE cozy mystery series, comprising six books; of the new LAURA FROST FBI suspense thriller, comprising nine books (and counting); of the new ELLA DARK FBI suspense thriller, comprising fourteen books (and counting); of the A YEAR IN EUROPE cozy mystery series, comprising nine books, of the AVA GOLD mystery series, comprising six books (and counting); of the RACHEL GIFT mystery series, comprising eight books (and counting); of the VALERIE LAW mystery series, comprising nine books (and counting); of the PAIGE KING mystery series, comprising six books (and counting); of the MAY MOORE mystery series, comprising nine books (and counting); the CORA SHIELDS mystery series, comprising three books (and counting); and of the NICKY LYONS mystery series, comprising three books (and counting).

An avid reader and lifelong fan of the mystery and thriller genres, Blake loves to hear from you, so please feel free to visit www.blakepierceauthor.com to learn more and stay in touch.

BOOKS BY BLAKE PIERCE

NICKY LYONS MYSTERY SERIES
ALL MINE (Book #1)
ALL HIS (Book #2)
ALL HE SEES (Book #3)

CORA SHIELDS MYSTERY SERIES
UNDONE (Book #1)
UNWANTED (Book #2)
UNHINGED (Book #3)

MAY MOORE SUSPENSE THRILLER
NEVER RUN (Book #1)
NEVER TELL (Book #2)
NEVER LIVE (Book #3)
NEVER HIDE (Book #4)
NEVER FORGIVE (Book #5)
NEVER AGAIN (Book #6)
NEVER LOOK BACK (Book #7)
NEVER FORGET (Book #8)
NEVER LET GO (Book #9)

PAIGE KING MYSTERY SERIES
THE GIRL HE PINED (Book #1)
THE GIRL HE CHOSE (Book #2)
THE GIRL HE TOOK (Book #3)
THE GIRL HE WISHED (Book #4)
THE GIRL HE CROWNED (Book #5)
THE GIRL HE WATCHED (Book #6)

VALERIE LAW MYSTERY SERIES
NO MERCY (Book #1)
NO PITY (Book #2)
NO FEAR (Book #3)
NO SLEEP (Book #4)
NO QUARTER (Book #5)
NO CHANCE (Book #6)

NO REFUGE (Book #7)
NO GRACE (Book #8)
NO ESCAPE (Book #9)

RACHEL GIFT MYSTERY SERIES
HER LAST WISH (Book #1)
HER LAST CHANCE (Book #2)
HER LAST HOPE (Book #3)
HER LAST FEAR (Book #4)
HER LAST CHOICE (Book #5)
HER LAST BREATH (Book #6)
HER LAST MISTAKE (Book #7)
HER LAST DESIRE (Book #8)

AVA GOLD MYSTERY SERIES
CITY OF PREY (Book #1)
CITY OF FEAR (Book #2)
CITY OF BONES (Book #3)
CITY OF GHOSTS (Book #4)
CITY OF DEATH (Book #5)
CITY OF VICE (Book #6)

A YEAR IN EUROPE
A MURDER IN PARIS (Book #1)
DEATH IN FLORENCE (Book #2)
VENGEANCE IN VIENNA (Book #3)
A FATALITY IN SPAIN (Book #4)

ELLA DARK FBI SUSPENSE THRILLER
GIRL, ALONE (Book #1)
GIRL, TAKEN (Book #2)
GIRL, HUNTED (Book #3)
GIRL, SILENCED (Book #4)
GIRL, VANISHED (Book 5)
GIRL ERASED (Book #6)
GIRL, FORSAKEN (Book #7)
GIRL, TRAPPED (Book #8)
GIRL, EXPENDABLE (Book #9)
GIRL, ESCAPED (Book #10)
GIRL, HIS (Book #11)

GIRL, LURED (Book #12)
GIRL, MISSING (Book #13)
GIRL, UNKNOWN (Book #14)

LAURA FROST FBI SUSPENSE THRILLER
ALREADY GONE (Book #1)
ALREADY SEEN (Book #2)
ALREADY TRAPPED (Book #3)
ALREADY MISSING (Book #4)
ALREADY DEAD (Book #5)
ALREADY TAKEN (Book #6)
ALREADY CHOSEN (Book #7)
ALREADY LOST (Book #8)
ALREADY HIS (Book #9)

EUROPEAN VOYAGE COZY MYSTERY SERIES
MURDER (AND BAKLAVA) (Book #1)
DEATH (AND APPLE STRUDEL) (Book #2)
CRIME (AND LAGER) (Book #3)
MISFORTUNE (AND GOUDA) (Book #4)
CALAMITY (AND A DANISH) (Book #5)
MAYHEM (AND HERRING) (Book #6)

ADELE SHARP MYSTERY SERIES
LEFT TO DIE (Book #1)
LEFT TO RUN (Book #2)
LEFT TO HIDE (Book #3)
LEFT TO KILL (Book #4)
LEFT TO MURDER (Book #5)
LEFT TO ENVY (Book #6)
LEFT TO LAPSE (Book #7)
LEFT TO VANISH (Book #8)
LEFT TO HUNT (Book #9)
LEFT TO FEAR (Book #10)
LEFT TO PREY (Book #11)
LEFT TO LURE (Book #12)
LEFT TO CRAVE (Book #13)
LEFT TO LOATHE (Book #14)
LEFT TO HARM (Book #15)

CHLOE FINE PSYCHOLOGICAL SUSPENSE SERIES
NEXT DOOR (Book #1)
A NEIGHBOR'S LIE (Book #2)
CUL DE SAC (Book #3)
SILENT NEIGHBOR (Book #4)
HOMECOMING (Book #5)
TINTED WINDOWS (Book #6)

KATE WISE MYSTERY SERIES
IF SHE KNEW (Book #1)
IF SHE SAW (Book #2)
IF SHE RAN (Book #3)
IF SHE HID (Book #4)
IF SHE FLED (Book #5)
IF SHE FEARED (Book #6)
IF SHE HEARD (Book #7)

THE MAKING OF RILEY PAIGE SERIES
WATCHING (Book #1)
WAITING (Book #2)
LURING (Book #3)
TAKING (Book #4)
STALKING (Book #5)
KILLING (Book #6)

RILEY PAIGE MYSTERY SERIES
ONCE GONE (Book #1)
ONCE TAKEN (Book #2)
ONCE CRAVED (Book #3)
ONCE LURED (Book #4)
ONCE HUNTED (Book #5)
ONCE PINED (Book #6)
ONCE FORSAKEN (Book #7)
ONCE COLD (Book #8)
ONCE STALKED (Book #9)
ONCE LOST (Book #10)
ONCE BURIED (Book #11)
ONCE BOUND (Book #12)
ONCE TRAPPED (Book #13)
ONCE DORMANT (Book #14)

ONCE SHUNNED (Book #15)
ONCE MISSED (Book #16)
ONCE CHOSEN (Book #17)

MACKENZIE WHITE MYSTERY SERIES
BEFORE HE KILLS (Book #1)
BEFORE HE SEES (Book #2)
BEFORE HE COVETS (Book #3)
BEFORE HE TAKES (Book #4)
BEFORE HE NEEDS (Book #5)
BEFORE HE FEELS (Book #6)
BEFORE HE SINS (Book #7)
BEFORE HE HUNTS (Book #8)
BEFORE HE PREYS (Book #9)
BEFORE HE LONGS (Book #10)
BEFORE HE LAPSES (Book #11)
BEFORE HE ENVIES (Book #12)
BEFORE HE STALKS (Book #13)
BEFORE HE HARMS (Book #14)

AVERY BLACK MYSTERY SERIES
CAUSE TO KILL (Book #1)
CAUSE TO RUN (Book #2)
CAUSE TO HIDE (Book #3)
CAUSE TO FEAR (Book #4)
CAUSE TO SAVE (Book #5)
CAUSE TO DREAD (Book #6)

KERI LOCKE MYSTERY SERIES
A TRACE OF DEATH (Book #1)
A TRACE OF MURDER (Book #2)
A TRACE OF VICE (Book #3)
A TRACE OF CRIME (Book #4)
A TRACE OF HOPE (Book #5)

Made in United States
North Haven, CT
30 May 2023

37172644R00105